Emily's Blues

A Fictionalized Autobiography

Based on a true story

By Connie Williams

Published: A Williams Acorn Publication
An imprint of AWAP
Correspondences addressed to cmae77@att.net

This is a work of fiction with literary elements and insights based on experience. Any references to real people in this work that resemble real persons, either living or dead; or to real places are intended only to give the work a setting in historical reality. Other names, characters, places, and incidents either are the product of the author's imagination, used fictitiously, and their resemblance, if any, to real-life social groups is entirely coincidental.

Front illustration by C. Williams
Back design © C-Mae Williams

Library of Congress TX 2 592 844
Copyright © 1989 by Williams, Connie: Emily's Blues
All rights reserved.

ISBN   978-0-692-63019-8 (13 font)

Printed in the United States of America 2016

The late Alex Haley:

"You really do have a compelling story that could be in competition with mine."

Union County Schools' personnel:

Ms. Williams expands upon a valuable lesson: young females must be taught how and when to say "NO" to sexual advances from males; especially ones who pave the feminine road with violence, alcoholism, drug abuse and neglect. Ms. Williams illustrates how easily and inevitably this occurs—her story is worth telling; her journey is relevant to many young women.

--Ann McAuley, Charlotte-Mecklenburg Schools:

"Though *Emily's Blues* is a work of fiction,
Ms. Williams has expertly
combined essential insights based on experience to help create
a lasting effect upon the reader."

--The late Dr. George Herrick, Professor of English. Emeritus
Los Angeles Valley College:

"Within the novel are realistic descriptions of
Emily's early life in Morristown,
the romance with Larry, the marriage
to Walter and the experiences in New York,
New Jersey, Washington, DC, and finally California."

By Connie Williams

Emily's Blues rereleased 2016

Green

Mama Allie's Talking Dogs in Fried Croakers

Hands
Mama You, Poetry

Emily's Dilemma, Stage play

John and Lila's Dance, a novel

QAK, QAK: What are we supposed to do? A novel expected 2020

Life: Through Grace Hope and Mercy: An inspirational testimony, expected 2018

Emily's Sequel, a novel expected 2019

Audacity, research prose expected 2019

Untied Shoelaces, a novel expected 2020

This book is dedicated to mothers, fathers, sons and daughters, and the loving memory of my Donna Lynne and Connie Maria.

CONTENTS

Prelude

*T*he part of the story some say that is the most compelling is the part that I'm too scared to tell. But I guess I can go ahead and tell it anyway. Maybe the folks that didn't notice me before won't notice me now. As a child I remember, my Uncle Andes saying, I moved like the wind because I arrived; I left sometimes without anyone ever knowing it. Right now it's cold outside. And the chill of the room is taking me back to an earlier time—a difficult one.

*F*ive months after my fifteenth birthday, my parents drove Walter Phifer and me across the North Carolina line to the Justice of the Peace in South Carolina to be married. I was going to have a baby— Walter's best friend Larry's child. Walter a nineteen year old, who lived in a big white house up the hill from our house, who I met through Larry just four months earlier, said he wanted my baby to have a father. He asked to marry me.

It was the warm month of October, 1959, and leaves fallen from tree branches covered the grounds. I wore one of Mama's old green cotton dresses that I found two days before, as I searched through the chifforobe drawers looking for a dress to wear, to get married in. I spent the next day cutting the seams open on the dress I found and pedaling that Sears sewing machine that sat in Mama's bedroom the same way I had seen her do, stitching up the seams to make the dress fit. I also found a wrinkled up white polyester flower on one of her old hats and ironed the wrinkles out after I ironed the dress. I pinned the flower on the dress to make it look pretty.

As the car glided pass Winchester Avenue and pass uptown going south to Highway 200, I sat quietly, and very close to Walter in the back seat, and I stiffened as my mind flashed back to a month earlier when my mama told me I needed to walk uptown to Dr. Clegg's office to have what she called a checkup—to see that the baby and I were all right.

I went to Dr. Clegg the local black doctor, an old man well into his seventies was more white than he was black, who had delivered me and all of my nine siblings right at home when we lived first on Seaboard Street and then on Fairley in Morristown.

So I automatically figured that Mama wanted him to deliver my child too. I thought of how his nurse gave me a gown that opened in the back; how she told me to pull my pants and underwear off and to climb up onto the examination table, and she placed a white sheet over my stomach and legs. My feet stuck out of the sheet, and she told me to put them into the stirrups at the end of the table. When Dr. Clegg came in, his nurse left the room. Being there alone, I felt afraid. But I felt comforted also because Mama said, "He will take care of you." So when he squeezed my breasts, put his fingers into my vagina, felt my stomach and then washed his hands in a sink, he returned to me and looked into my ears with an instrument—then he too left the room; although I had never gone to a doctor before, I felt instinctively, that he was doing what Mama said— examining me—doing what a doctor is suppose to do for his patient. In a moment, he returned to the room and stood at the end of the examination table as I laid there.

At the brink, in my mind of remembering lying there on the examination table, Daddy mashed the car breaks instantly and my thoughts were jarred to the present as the car's tires screech and he avoided driving through a pile of leaves in the middle of the highway. The car pulled off again and at the next light, we saw the Justice of the Peace sign. I was glad because I didn't want to think of Dr. Clegg again.

The ceremony at the Justice of the Peace was quick and matter-of-factly. Daddy paid the magistrate after he pronounced us husband and wife. Walter kissed me, Mama and Daddy hugged us both. We returned to the car for the ride back to Morristown, North Carolina, to Mom and Dad's. As we rode back, Walter wrapped his arms around me and held on to me tightly; I felt his hot breath on my neck and I remember thinking about my life before he came along.

I thought about how I couldn't wait to leave my parents' house, even if it meant marrying Walter. I decided that I wouldn't ever even *look* back. I was determined to escape and avoid living in the place of my early youth. There were so many of us children. It was hard to take care of all of us. All we had was a child's very basic needs: *something* to eat and a roof to keep the rain and the snow off our heads. I thought about at age thirteen, the night my mother and I sat putting little bits of cheese on a mousetrap catching and piling the rodents that kept running about the house, biting holes in our bread. The bed bugs and roaches slept and thrived more than we did. So I had many reasons for marrying someone who I hardly knew.

I could hardly wait to leave the place. Ironically the filth that filled every crack and crevice was not because of a lack of the effort or neglect to clean it where my mother or I were concerned. Poor Mama, she labored for long hours in the white folk's houses, and then in her own. I had seen her on many a winter morning bent over a large tin tub scrubbing dirty clothes on a washboard until the spots were removed long before dawn and "Shout It Out" was on the market. In essence, Mama couldn't keep up with the messiness of all of her children, but she really tried, and I never saw a woman more proud when on Saturday night she was all dressed up after her efforts to clean the place up and put a meal on the table, knowing Daddy was soon coming in from work. No! The filth in our house existed from an evolution of *not having*—of *poverty*. To me the only

9

possible way to fix it, the only means of fumigation and elimination of such ills was to put a bulldozer to the place leveling it to the ground with hopes of destroying, forever, the pests dwelling within.

There was a problem even with this idea. In neighborhoods such as these, the pests simply scurried through the grass to find new refuge, build nest, lay eggs right next door. And when the dust settled and a new house was built as soon as the lights went out the pest crept into the new house.

My mind flashed back again to Dr. Clegg standing at the end of the examination table. Iron–hand Mom never knew what he did to me after the examination—she didn't give me any money to pay the *good doctor* for his services. As I laid there after his examination; suddenly, in an instant, a quick second, I felt something being pushed inside me again. This time it wasn't his finger as before or an instrument, he was pushing his *shriveled up "self"* into my vagina. He popped it in and I felt some warm sticky fluid inside of me and then he jerked it out—it happened so fast I could not move. I lay there very still with my head turned away and—not knowing what to do. As Dr. Clegg put his *"self"* back into his pants and before he left the room he told me, "You can get up and put your clothes on." He said, "Next time wear a dress." He took advantage *of a poor little girl with no money*. After he left the room, I climbed down from the examination table, pulled my panties on and felt them get wet and sticky with semen.

Afterwards, I walked home from Dr. Clegg's office across the railroad tracks pass Larry's house, the father of my unborn child. The shame I felt for what Dr. Clegg had done to me; the pity I held inside my mind was almost unbearable for how Larry had betrayed me.

The smell oozing up of the wet sticky stuff crept into my nostrils—only God knows why I did not vomit. I never told Mama or Daddy what happened—I was too afraid. I've carried that secret inside of me until my mentally revealing it now. I just didn't know who would believe me. Besides, no one wanted to protect a poor little girl with nothing, not a winter coat, not a new dress to get married in, *not even the sound advice of a parent.*

A man that does not teach his daughters about the "ways and woes" of males does them a grave injustice. A girl not taught at a young age to stand her own ground and say NO— NO to the male's seductive advances is at the mercy of the Beasts.

It's really funny, but my memory is *almost* completely obliterated of my eighteenth birthday when one becomes idealistically an adult. What's more, I don't remember a celebration, a gift, or what's even more devastating, where I was at the time—I mean whether I was in New York, New Jersey, Washington or North Carolina. I remember vaguely a party and fried chicken, picture taking at some lady's house (I later learned that she was my husband Walter's girlfriend) in my hometown, but I just can't remember how old I was at the time, whether I was eighteen, nineteen or twenty.

It saddens me when I have to think of life—it is impossible—the pain. It seems that my teenage years had been spent waiting, wishing, praying, and hoping— all passive actions in a motion-filled society; and yet with this passivity I would continually find my belly swollen big with a new fetus and feeling absolutely helpless.

One day, some years later, when I was still very young, I managed to pull together enough nerve to ask the lady behind the desk at the California Welfare office if I could use some of funds to go to school, get an education and become a teacher. She pulled her eyeglasses down from two steel blue eyes causing goose bumps to form on the back of my neck, and I became ashamed to have asked such a question as her stare penetrated my soul when she replied coldly, ***"That's absolutely unreal."***

And here we all are, endeavoring to go on, to breathe this air and maintain this palpitation of the heart. We really have no choice. As Marilyn French puts it, we go around, around and around. But the cycle to which she refers is not synonymous to the vicious cycle of life I experienced. The question now in my mind is: could the courses of my life have been changed? Could the experiences have been different? What if I had been given strength—the strength of a parent's words passed on to the child, and the nurtured protection of a parent to the child; what if I had the wisdom of my parents given to me in their advice? What if I had been instructed to say ***"NO!"*** to Larry, and ***"NO!"*** to Walter?

Part I
Grits

*I*t **was late winter of 1959,** and there was snow on the tree branches in Morristown, North Carolina, a little town of only fourteen thousand, quiet, slow-paced people. These deep rooted people, who imitated the sophisticated the   mannerisms   of more   important people   on Sunday, but on most occasions during the congregation of the family on Saturday night, they would slip back into their real world, and the "jibber jive" was sure to start.

On the north side of this little town across the tracks in Bright Town, a member of the family would say "Boy you're sho crazy." He would reply, "Chile, I ain't crazy. If I was crazy, would I be able to do this?" He would dance his dance and the family would laugh and applaud him. He would then say, I'm not crazy, I'm just feelin good."

And on the south side of town known as Bottleneck, on a Saturday night, a man would sit on his front porch, drink a pint of liquor and say, "Well, dam-it, hell I'm high." He would lean back in his chair, shake his head from side to side as hard as he could almost making his lip flap in the wind, pick up his pistol and talk like the man he'd seen in the movies. "I'm gone kill me somebody tonight." Someone would ask, "Neigh who you gone kill, Boy?" His reply would be, "Wait till in the morning, you-ah-read-bout-it."

There was comradeship in Bright Town and Bottleneck. Those of us who lived in Bright Town lived within a perfect square of protection. Or at least it seemed that way. June Kannapolis, Old Lady Dridges, Ms. Matthews Homely and my grandmother, AJ covered this complete territory of news. If you were from across the tracks, you had better sense than to say anything about anyone from Bright Town and let it get back to them. These ladies knew all of the comings and goings—when the iceman came, when the water man left the lid off the meter, what time the mail arrived and whether Sister Odessa paid the premium of her life coverage policy to the insurance man. And those from Bright Town had better think twice before saying anything about the people who lived in Bottleneck. These ladies had connections all over town. If Old Lady Dridges got hold of a story and happen to miss out on any part of it, she could put together a tale that she started to make up two minutes before it was time for the noon whistle to blow down at the sewing mill. She could tell it in between smacking her poisonous deadly blue gums, spitting out snuff that landed a fly on the porch flat on his back three feet away, throw in an "I swear 'fo' God" and make you believe it by the time the mill whistle sounded.

Anything that was said at eight o'clock that morning would have been repeated twelve different times with twenty-four different endings by eight o'clock that night at the supper table. Any tale that Old

Lady failed to verbally resolve would be instantly picked up by Mae Raleigh, who sat on her front porch from sunup to sundown chewing on Milk of Magnesia squares. She was sure to summons a passerby to engage in some "child you know what I heard" chitchat, in an attempt to get the "ups" on Old Lady Dridges.

Early Saturdays sometimes brought with it rituals of expectation and excitement. We looked forward to Mama's shopping at Mangum's, the corner grocery store where she was allowed to running tab for groceries. She brought home that large can of thick maple syrup and two pounds of bologna meat because it was pancakes, fried potatoes and bologna night. In the kitchen we beat batter, diced spuds and heated grease till it was good and hot to fry the potatoes, while our parents dressed up, and Mama dabbed on talcum powder behind closed doors. They were preparing themselves to go out to the Royal Garden jute joint.

When the food was ready, we piled onto the sofa under a thick blanket to watch wrestling with Gorgeous George on the black and white TV. We "sopped" pancakes in syrup that ran down our chin as we cheered when George removed his gold hairpins from his curly blond hair. By twelve midnight when the public broadcasting station signed off with the National Anthem, we piled into beds underneath the blankets and the winter coats, fulfilled with the sweet taste of happiness that Saturday brought.

By two or three o'clock Sunday morning, when our parents returned home from the club, they entered the front porch with its shabby step. It led them into the cold and dark isolated rooms that gave no sign of life at night except for the stench of urine and the number of winter coats that warmed our breathing bodies that lay in beds. But the doors to the rooms were closed during the day to keep the rest of the house warm. Right before it was time for us children to go to bed, the doors to these rooms were flung open so heat could circulate through them.   And once we were in bed and under the covers and the coats, the doors were closed again. Then these rooms became connected only by the walls which brought forth the indistinguishable commotion from the voices of the couple that lay in bed, which could be heard in the adjoining rooms on either side.

The passion which moved the couple rose to a peak and became one with our enthralled, listening, breathing young minds that lay in the beds. The older minds were enraged by the every Saturday night affair. Perhaps the young minds were thrilled by the rapture. I supposed to them, the familiarity of the sounds was reminiscent of an end-of-the-week celebration.

During the winter mornings the family gathered around the coal heater in Mama and Daddy's little two by four, chilly and damp bedroom to eat a bowl of grits for breakfast. By then Mama was growing fat from the Saturday night celebration. I was very observant. So I stared at my mother's slightly protruding belly. When she caught me looking, as usual, Mama said exactly what was on her mind. "What ah-you –lookin-at-Emily? Eat-yo-grits." I was perplexed by my mother's anger. It seemed that she was not ready for the family to know that she was expecting another baby. But I didn't need to be told. I possessed that sixth sense that told me about the bulge underneath Mama's sweater. I loved my mother, Martha, and would never cross her, so I looked in another direction and finished eating my bowl of warm grits.

Within five months, in April, when the red birds begin to sing, and the morning-glory with its various deep hues of purple, pink and yellow spread over the hill, I stayed home from school to cook the grits for my brothers and sisters while Dr. Clegg embraced the wringing hands of the agonized patient that lay in bed in the adjourning room. Once the grit were done, I buttered them and fed the siblings and sat watching them eat and thinking to myself at the kitchen table. I thought even though this was April, Daddy would need to get some more coal for the heater since there was going to be a newborn baby in the house. As I sat waiting with my sisters and brothers at the kitchen table, suddenly they all stopped eating to smile to the "Eeeeee" of a newborn baby's cry. We all knew in our hearts that a new sister or brother had arrived to join the family. We were anxious to see for ourselves.

I imagined Dr. Clegg embraced the wringing hands of the agonized patient that laid in bed in the room from where the sound had come. He cut the umbilical cord. Thomas, her husband who had been sitting at the end of the bed with worried eyes and patience, approached his wife and leaned over her to kiss her head.

I understood what they were doing, thinking and saying: Thank you doctor. Fine job you did there. She wasn't in labor long. Sure am glad it's over. She was a good patient. Fine boy you got yourself there, they were saying-- talking in low voices because they knew children were listening.

It was now pass seven o'clock a.m. And although it was winter, the sun came piercing through the window. I moved from the kitchen and my sisters and I stood at the door where we heard the baby's cry. Cautiously I asked, "Can I see it Mama? Is it a girl or a boy?" Hoping deep inside that it would be another girl. I thought of how easy little girls were to care for. They wet their diapers in the middle, not up front where the pee wet the tail of the T-shirt. And when they got older, they didn't go around tearing the heads off your dolls just to see what made the eyes and mouths open and close.

My father, Thomas, cracked the door, stuck his head out and said, "It's a boy. But you kids can't come in yet. Emily, see after these kids."

"Come on y'all," I said to my four younger sisters who stood at the door and with me returned to the kitchen.

"What's Daddy and the doctor doing?" asked Jimmy, who sat at the table eating breakfast with his brother Greg. Elizabeth, Brenda and a younger sister Alice who was a quiet girl, now sat at the table with them.

Before I could answer, "Daddy talkin to da docta, and he told us we couldn't come in," said Rosie, who was now the second to the youngest child. Rosie, at three years old could talk well for her age. The relatives said that she talked quickly to get out of the way of the baby that was coming. She stood against the kitchen door, which led to the living room with one leg crossed over the other and a thumb in her mouth. "Daddy don' give that baby he bottle. Ain't he Jimmy?" asked Rosie, as she waddled over to the table and climbed up in a chair again.

The two brothers laughed and rose from the table to put their plates into the kitchen sink. "We've got to go," said Jimmy. The two boys put on their coats and hats for school. "We'll see the baby when we come home for lunch. Won't we Emily?" He pulled his brother by the arm. "Hope Mama won't name him Russell. He might look like old man Russell that cleans up at the school." Jimmy and Greg started to laugh as they left for school.

I turned to my three younger sisters who were school age and said, "Get on your coats so you can go now, too." I thought, I am the second to the oldest sibling, and I must care for the house, my mother, my sisters and brothers – I am the adult now. There is neither time for bickering nor incisiveness. Not now. Not when there is so much to do. I thought, although Grandma AJ says I am a small-undernourished figure of thirteen, I stiffened with authority. "Here, put your arm in here." I said to my sisters Elizabeth, then Brenda and Alice as I prepared the girls to go out into the brisk morning air. I was glad they had not put up any resistance. Sending my sisters on their way, and before closing the door to the fresh violet smell of oncoming spring, I was greeted at the door by the old face of a woman, whom I love, wrapped in a coat and wearing a scarf on her head.

"How's yo mama?" My grandmother, AJ, said almost in a chopped up whisper that came from her shivering body. She rushed into the room and over to the huge oil stove that sat in the middle of the living room. She laid her icicle hands over the top to melt away the cold. She stood there.

Searching her down with careful precaution, wanting to meet her with equal eyes, I answered, "Mama had a boy. Daddy wouldn't let me see it yet," as I stood by the door listening again to the murmuring voices inside as my grandmother warmed herself. The two of us became one in thought in the stillness which overtook the living room.

"Lord have mercy," uttered the old voice from a broken figure that stood by the heater, as she shook her head from side to side. She had come to stand by her daughter in childbirth – to know that all was well. She had come so many times before. So many times before she had prayed and whispered, Lord have mercy for her daughter who was giving birth in a quiet room, with the doctor standing on one side of her bed, and her husband sitting at the foot watching with wide careful eyes. She knew that her son-in-law, Thomas, loved her daughter, Martha, and was a hard-working man for his family. The old woman stood still by the heater with her mind on yesterday when she became grandmother to the first born: Ruth, then came Emily, Jimmy, Greg, Elizabeth, Brenda, Alice and Rosie who was her grandmother's heart, then Cam, a two year old who was still asleep in bed, and now the new born. As she stood there, she thought of Ruth, the oldest, who was already out into the world trying to earn her own board and keep at fifteen, and trying to go to school. "Thank God Almighty that she is a stout and healthy girl. And I sho hope that the Lord will take care of her, so she won't have no babies – at least not before she finishes school, and get herself a husband to take care of her."

The old woman stood near the heater, and there the big warm machine had become her husband in her quiet meditation as she leaned on its warm, strong shoulders. She thought, "Lord Jesus, you took my Claude 'bout five years ago when Alice was a baby, and my daughter moved next door to me. Time sho do fly."

At that instant, the old woman was brought back to the present when she heard the door open, and Dr. Clegg and Thomas came out of the room with gleaming eyes of mutual admiration, the father proud of his baby – a doctor proud of his work.

"Well, Thomas she'll be all right." Dr. Clegg reached for his coat and hat that laid on the sofa. He puts them on and buttons up his coat.

"Thank you doctor and I'll be in to see you on Saturday." Thomas walked toward the door to open it for the doctor.

As Dr. Clegg picked up his black bag and prepared to go out of the door, he turned and said, "Now don't let that old lady fuss over the baby and spoil him." He smiled at Addie and then walked away.

Addie, no longer daydreaming about the past, although not completely letting go, turned her attention to Thomas and the doctor. Addie deeply despised Dr. Clegg, and she thought him a fool for referring to her as old. She thought, "Why he's just as old as I *is*. He thinks he's young, runnin round wid dem young women. Thinkin folks don't know bout it. Shoot he's crazy. I got my connections. I see folks everyday dat's been all over dis town—even up yonder where he *do* his doctoring. Dey comes by here and tells me bout him and how he be carrin on up dah wid them "poor" gals he spose to be takin care of. One of dese days he'll have a heart attack and die."

Thomas saw the doctor off and greeted Addie at the heater breaking into her thoughts. "Hi you, Miss Addie?" He said to her tenderly.

She came to total consciousness and answered, "I'll do. How's Martha?"

"She's sleeping now. The baby's a boy." Their eyes met, the two generations, and she passed him to transfer her attention to her daughter and the newborn.

I still stood at the heater. I greeted my father with the adult concern I felt he needed. "Daddy, you want some grits?"

"Yeah Emily, did you make some bread?"

"Yeah Daddy." I loved my father with all of my heart. As usual when I prepared his plate, it was done with care and concern, like a doctor is suppose to care for his patient, or a florist arranging his flowers. Freed from time, preoccupied in thought to please my dad, I placed his meal on the table in front of him. I asked, "Daddy, do you want me to stay home from school tomorrow?"

"Naw, you better go on to school tomorrow. I'll try to get Miss Addie to stay with your mama." He went on about eating his breakfast.

I would have gladly stayed home if he had asked me. I would do mostly anything my father asked me to do. And without speaking another word, I went on with my work. I cleaned the table, removing the dishes and placing them into the sink. I washed, dried them and put them away. I scoured the stove and then swept the kitchen floor. I removed a pack of pinto beans from the cupboard and measured out three cups, then picked the rocks from them, washed them added a slice of fat back, and put them into a large pot with water and placed it on the stove to cook the beans for supper.

I turned to the living room now and straightened the quilt that covered the sofa. Toys and shoes had been left on the floor. I picked them up and then carried them to the room where they belonged. I placed the shoes in the boys' room. Afterward I made the boys' bed and swept their linoleum floor. The drawers in their dresser had been left open with clothes hanging from them. These, too, I arranged and closed.

The toys were placed in the cardboard toy box in the girls' room. I picked up the clothes from the floor and put them in the four-drawer bureau. The mattress that Ruth, Elizabeth and Alice slept on was wet. I placed my hand into the tear to rearrange the cotton in the mattress. Then I folded the sheet down in the middle of the bed so the sunlight from the window would strike the mattress and dry it before night. I made the bed where I slept with Brenda. I went to my mother now and the newborn.

Growing up as the second to the oldest child of eleven children, I didn't receive my fair share of attention. And after we became teenagers, my oldest sister Ruth was gone most of the time either working or off with her friends. So with Mom and Dad working most of the time too, obviously the responsibilities of the house and other siblings became mine. I didn't mind; I didn't complain; I just did it. At thirteen when most girls were doing the girlie thing—experiencing with makeup, talking on the telephone about boys (by the way, we didn't have a telephone), going to the movies, spending time with friends, most of my time was spent working at home: planning and cooking meals, washing clothes and cleaning after my siblings—totally domesticated. I arrived at school late on many a morning because I really enjoyed cleaning the girl's and the boy's room.

Fixing up the place made me feel important—*this was all I knew*.

****

The next morning, I sat at my desk next to Alvin in Mrs. Carlson's eighth-grade class. Alvin was a small-framed boy with sunken cheeks who lived across the tracks. His pale hollow cheeks revealed a pleasure from my presence that was unmistakably noticeable. He often pulled my braids and punched me lightly, when we were on the play yard at recess to get my attention. This morning he simply sat smiling at me. He hoped for some mutual sign of acceptance, but this morning was no different from the others. I frowned when our eyes met, as though I tasted bitter chocolate. And the smile on Alvin's face quickly faded and resumed its usual hollowness.

The two of us were called to attention like two soldiers by Mrs. Carlson when she asked. "Emily, how do you tell a boy baby from a girl baby?"

Becoming flushed with embarrassment, I sat there with the stares and snickers of my classmates upon me. Curiously, I thought—knowing there was a good reason for this question. I knew exactly from where this question had come. The classroom was silent. They all watched and waited. Or was it curiosity? No, I decided. No—I thought. Mrs. Carlson knows I wasn't in school yesterday—my mama just had *another* baby—she knows—they all know that I *do* know about such things. But like a child taught to be seen and not heard, I didn't speak. I sat silently. I was reluctant to speak for fear my answer would not be acceptable—I wanted to tell them: anyone knows that all you have to do is look inside the baby's diaper at its private parts. But I didn't want to let on that I knew more than the other girls who didn't have to change the diapers of their younger sisters and brothers. Therefore, I took the safe path, and in my silence I felt superior.

Part 11
School Was Out

*T*he month of May brought its usual **abundance** of Daisies and Lilies that spread over the fields, but more importantly I became fourteen, and early in June school was out. When the school doors opened, my classmates and I burst out, like horses set free of our controlling ropes. Our steady feet carried us to the favorite places—the play yards, the ball fields, the back porches, the fishing ponds and the local ice cream, soda pop and hamburger joints. We came with the thunder of laughter echoing in the air.

During the hot months of summer, I spent my time in shorts and shirts, building crafts with my hands at the Westchester Recreation Center handicraft meetings from nine until twelve o'clock on Mondays and Wednesdays. These meetings were my main social involvement. I occasionally attended Sunday school at True Love Baptist Church. My irregular attendance caused the regular church goers, like June Kannapolis, a Deaconess, to one day ask me if I was coming as a member or a visitor creating an embarrassment in my mind and pain in her heart. It caused my feet to become lead and the isle seemed such a long distance from the door, so much that I began to slide quickly and as unnoticeable as an ant crawling across the sand into a back row seat. Christians like June Kannapolis was on the usher-board, the chorus and taught Sunday school. She just thought it was a Cardinal sin if a member did not attend church every Sunday no matter what the circumstances; after all she was there seven days a week and all day on the Sabbath. No one ever thought that perhaps the reason I wasn't in regular attendance was because I didn't have clothes to wear to church. June Kannapolis was sure to take all of the church business/goings on back to the neighborhood to Old Lady Dridges, to Grandma AJ who dressed in her pull over the head apron with frills, and to Mae Raleigh. They gathered at early evening at Mae Raleigh's front porch talking some gossip chewing it up and spitting it out until dusk dark.

Growing tired of the humiliation of the church saints pointing the finger, I decided to pursue my trust in God Almighty in the little local Catholic Church on Winchester. There I could attend Bible school or church and feel a sense of belongingness. I could be involved in something other than the Saturday morning rummage where, if I were lucky, I could find clothes donated by upper-class whites. And at Bible school meetings, the Nuns and Father Roberts liked me. They always put me in charge of the Kool-Aid and cookies at refreshment time. There, no one asked me if I was a member or just visiting. The Nuns and Father Roberts just seemed to be glad by revealing a warm smile with a friendly "Good morning" when I managed to show up.

Although school was recently over for the summer, when the youths gathered together the usual conversations were still centered on the classrooms and the teachers of Westchester, before they broke into activity groups.

Handicraft meetings allowed for eventful creativity. Members sewed, upholstered, made ceramics projects and created art. There was also a free hour of music and dancing after snacks at the end of each meeting. I liked dancing; sometime at home, when I wasn't cooking and cleaning, I pretended to be a ballerina and danced around and around on my toes. At Handicraft, I felt uninhibited and enjoyed being with other peers of my age. Most of the members that attended were the neighborhood youths, teenagers who saw each other and hung together during the hot days of summer.

At night we sat out on porches talking, as Grandma AJ would say, young folks talk and swing their legs off the edges of porches, gazing up at the stars and wondered about the heavens. Most days and night weren't much different from the next. Occasionally there was a birthday party held in a back yard. The young folks got together and sometimes did something wild like sneaking in and stealing the watermelons from the white folks' watermelon patch. The melons were still warm from the heat of the hot summer day, but they cracked them open and ate them at the party anyway. There was nothing like sweet, ripe watermelon still a little warm right out of the garden.

One day of summer seemed to fade into the next. But on this particular day at the Handicraft meeting something was different. There were two different faces, and they seemed to be studying me from across the room. Catching the eyes of him and his friend watching, I could feel myself blushing, as a baby who does what is expected of him by his parents and is praised.

According to Uncle Andes, my cousin Barbara's father, I was referred to as beautiful, and even I noticed how the young boys usually reacted to my charm just as Alvin, my classmate and the new, older ones like Larry and Sean who had come to the meeting. Mae Raleigh said my face was a blend of my mother's soft mixed white, Native American and African American features and the dominant ones of my ethnically mixed father of the same structure. According to the locals, it was an oval diamond face with pointed nose and delicate lips-- eyes dark as shinny marbles—so dark they were almost black surrounded by long, silky black, straight eyelashes. My brows I painted darker with a burnt match stem smutted from the stove pipe slanted up into a natural arch were seen as stunning against my brown skin—that skin called light by many and protected by staying indoors to guard it from the hot North Carolina summer sun.

I sat with a cousin Barbara and a group of Bright Town and Bottle Neck girls on one side of the Westchester center on this hot day in mid July, I must have made a pretty- as- a- doll picture. My red, yellow and green floral print shirt I found rummaging through the give-away clothes at the Catholic Church perfectly matched the red Bermuda shorts and the red moccasins given to me by a teacher when I performed in a school dance a month earlier. My flowery shirttail cut top hung flattering over and hid the small breast and tiny waist underneath. But for all the carefree happiness my smile suggested, my true spirit was carefully concealed. The dark eyes in the agreeable face were unsure, and shy, surrendering clearly different from my colorful external appearance. I wasn't outgoing and "knowing" like my peers. I was totally aware that *I had nothing*.

Finally, the figure of a handsome boy of seventeen, whose face was yellow and smooth as a banana skin, walked slowly across the floor, moved in my direction. Everyone watched.

He walked right up to me and asked, "Your name is Emily isn't it?"

I looked at him in amazement and quickly lowered my eyes to the floor. All I could say was a timid, "Yes." I wanted to say more. I wanted to ask questions, like how did you know or who told you my name. But I couldn't. I didn't want to seem silly, talking silly eighth grade talk. The kind of talk that causes a boy to say, she sure is dumb talk when they're talking to each other away from the girls. But then I remembered that I had been promoted to the ninth grade. But still I knew I didn't have much experience on such matters as knowing what boys talked about. All I knew was when my cousins and I from across town from Bent Hill sometimes got together, they did talk about boys. My older cousins from across the highway said they knew what boys did and what they talked about— usually girls and what girls were and were not and what they liked and didn't like. The conversation floated into my thoughts and was interrupted.

"Let's dance," he said.

Remembering the way I felt once when I, caught unexpectedly, the sight of a shooting star and for a brief moment was unable to breathe, I stood and the two of us moved across the floor to choose a spot to dance. The jukebox was playing a loud blues song, "I Want to Walk You Home"; some couples were dancing close shuffling across the floor. Larry took me into his arms, encircling my waist with one arm while I placed one hand on his shoulder and held my head close to his chest. I had watched couples slow dance, but I myself had tried it only twice—once at my cousin's birthday party and again at the after-school sock hop. My mind quickly flashed back to the time that I stood on top of my father's feet as he held my hands and danced around the living room when I was a little girl. I felt comfortable then. But now I did not feel altogether comfortable in this situation—dancing with *this* boy.

He whispered in my ear, "I'm Larry, do you remember me?" And before I could answer, he continued, "My mother introduced us one Saturday when you and some other girls were over to the house practicing your dance for the May Day Program." His words made me remember. He went on, "Do you have a boyfriend?"

Feeling the strangeness of warmth rush through my body like water stirring in a lake, I hesitated for a while turning the words over in my mind before answering. I finally replied, "No, I don't." I wasn't sure.

Larry seemed to feel good about the way he smiled, held and twirled me gloriously about the floor. As we danced, I was trying to remember when we met, seeing him with his mother knowing she was a teacher at Westchester school; this gave me a good feeling inside too.

As we moved together I thought he was the best dancer in the world. Not once did he step on my feet like the boy did when they clumsily danced at her cousin's birthday party. I decided without any hesitation that Larry was wonderful. From what I had seen when he asked me to dance, he seemed to have the most beautiful eye that I had ever seen. And he was nice too, not like Hal Johnson, who tried to kiss me two days ago while we stood on the school playground. He couldn't find my mouth, kissing me on the nose and I ran home so he wouldn't try it again, even though I was thrilled by it and wanted to tell someone about it. I figured all girls got kissed sooner or later. They were always getting kissed on television and in the movies.

Handicraft at Westchester center ended, and everyone was starting to leave, laughing and talking together along the way, saying our goodbyes.

Larry walked up behind me and before he spoke, I sensed his presence. I wanted him to come nearer. He came closer this time beside me and asked, "Can I walk you home?"

I imagined Larry could see my grin, revealing the white teeth against my light tan skin. I answered, "Okay."

It was a hot day in mid-July, and the air held a sweet fragrance of roses and gardenias, like the back yard of a peach orchard, when the fruit is ripe and sweet, dripping with the flavorful juices. The sun shone brightly from a clear Carolina-blue sky. As Larry and I strolled in the direction my house, the two of us sometimes paused for a brief, but friendly chat about school, movies and our peers. Larry was a senior, three grades ahead of me in high school in the same class with my oldest sister, Ruth. He was from the Bright Town side of town too.

Larry put his arms around my shoulder wanting to draw me near, and I turned out of his control. "Why are you running from me?" he asked with a quick, seemingly hoarse laugh.

I had stopped to pick some little forget-me-nots that grew around the edge of a tree in the schoolyard. I picked them one-by-one and as I stood, I plucked the little white frills that surrounded the flowers, saying, "He loves me, he loves me not." Moderately ignoring Larry, but gaining his attention all the more, I responded, "I'm not running from you."

Larry came up to me and put one hand on both of my shoulders. Drawing me closer to him, he held me and attempted to kiss my lips. But I moved—turning my head toward the ground. He looked at me and let out a loud laugh. He then held me tightly. I had never been held this way before— not by anyone. It felt warm, and I could smell his cologne. I felt cared for and needed— loved. With our spirits high we wandered on towards my house down the street from the school in Bright Town.

Larry asked, "Have you ever had a boyfriend before?" It was for this precise question that Larry was lingering with a ninth grader on this July day. He confessed, "I think you're very pretty." It seemed and I imagined in his heart of hearts that he meant it. But more than that, I thought, he knows I am innocent. Yes, I am innocent.

I glanced at him. I hesitated and pondered what my answer should be about this boyfriend question... I didn't want Larry to think that I knew nothing about boys. "Yes, I had a boyfriend before, once, for about a month." I said. Inside I knew I was lying. And after saying it, I wanted to take it all back—to change my answer, to say "NO." I wanted to tell the truth. I had been taught to always tell the truth—the Sunday-school teacher said, until it hurt. The Lord blessed honest people. At least this is what I remembered Reverend Bittle had said in church. And I remembered his words, even the way he looked when he said it—kind of stern and stiff, like all preachers that I knew of when they were preaching the Holy words.

My thoughts floated to a conversation I had once with my mother. My mother told me that it was all right for a girl to have a boyfriend. But she said the Lord didn't want his children doing thing against the Holy word because that would be a sin. When she said this, she showed me a picture of a naked woman with her legs sprawled open. **It** was when I was eleven--when I ***"started."***

****

It was 5:30 p.m. when Larry and I arrived and I opened the door of my house amusing that the living room was quiet and drained of the patter of feet that usually dwelled within. Jimmy, Greg, Elizabeth, Brenda and Alice played in the backyard; while Rosie, Cam and Lewis were being kept next door at Grandma AJ's. The air was hot and stuffy as we entered.

Larry sat down on the torn sofa that was hidden underneath a purple quilt. I went directly to the bathroom, two doors away to check the neatness of my hair and face. Putting my hand up to my lips where Larry had wanted to kiss me, I smiled because I was so glad to have Larry with me to receive his attention.

I thought how handsome he looked in his brown khaki pants and yellow short-sleeve shirt. I felt proud, and opening the door of the bathroom, I walked lightheartedly back into the room where Larry was and sat down beside him on the sofa.

"Where have you been—putting make-up on your face?" He asked as he grabbed both of my shoulders with his hands to turn me to face him. I giggled. Larry seemed to want desperately to show me how he cared for me. He found his way to my lips and kissed them gently. This time I didn't attempt to move away. I felt helpless as a melting Popsicle in the hot sun.

Suddenly, the sound of the front door opening surprised the two of us, and Larry jumped to sit up straight. I couldn't remember how or when I had lain down, but I struggled up pulling at my shorts and straightening my hair simultaneously. I sat silently as my mother entered the door and stood smiling and somewhat questioningly at my new friend.

I didn't see much of Larry after that afternoon. I continued to attend handicraft classes regularly. I would linger around after class to see if he would drop in. He never did.

Feeling somewhat hurt, and remembering the way I felt when he had kissed me, I made up my mind not to allow my friends to see me carrying a long, sad look on my face, not since I thought that they were all wondering about what had happened between us.

****

School started again in September during the hot days of Indian summer, and I looked excitedly toward being a ninth grader. Ninth grade meant high school at Westchester High. All of the new high school students were meeting in the auditorium for orientation on the first day of school. My cousin, Barbara from the Bent Hill side of town would be attending school with me this year. I saw her when she entered the auditorium.

Barbara was all dresses up in a cool-looking yellow cotton dress and matching yellow and brown belt. She and I were the same age. She stood one inch taller than me, five feet two. She was an only child, and her parents, Uncle Andes and Aunt Teddy thought the sun and moon rose on their daughter. Barbara had what everyone called "big legs", long thick coal black hair and a bottom lip that protruded like Sophia Lauren's when she pouted.

Barbara and I were as close as cousin could be living in different areas in Morristown. Barbara grew up with her aunts, uncles and cousins on Bent Hill near our grandparents on our fathers' side. Our grandfather, Reverend Jones was a Methodist minister, and when we were younger we usually saw each other on Sunday at the "Big House" after church for the traditional fried chicken dinner with our grandmother's green-apple deep dish pie—huge green apples pulled right from the trees in their yard.

All of the cousins made a big fuss over Barbara. In fact, she was spoiled. Her mother even allowed her to drink beer when she was growing up, when she begged Aunt Teddy so hard, and just kept repeating, "Mama, I want some beer! Mama I want some beer!" Finally Aunt Teddy said, "Barbara Anne, my God." She had to give in to keep the girl quiet. That would not have been Martha. I knew better than to try that with her, about her beer. She would have back-handed me across the lips for asking once.

Some of the guys at school said Barbara was the best looking girl at Westchester High. "Hey, Barbara," I said giving her a big, wide smile. I hadn't seen my cousin in a matter of months. Not since Handicraft.

Returning the smile, Barbara came over to me and said, "You look cute. Did you make your skirt and blouse?" Barbara knew that I made most of the skirts and blouses I wore whenever I could straighten and curl someone's hair to earn a dollar or babysit or wash dishes for someone and then walk downtown to Woolworth and purchase a piece of cloth.

"Uh huh," I returned. We both spent some time looking around at the other students. I continued, "Do you know who your teacher will be this year?" But before Barbara was able to answer, "I hope we will be together in the same classroom. Don't you?" I said.
I squeezed my hand nervously, hoping to be assigned to the same room that my cousin was assigned to. She answered nervously, "Yes, I do too girl."

"Heard you been talking to Larry." Barbara turned and winked to Mildred and Silver our best friends, who were making their way hurriedly to join the two. They all huddled around me impatiently waiting for my response.

Inside my mind and my heart, I didn't really want to talk about it, but with the three waiting for my answer, I knew I had to. "He walked me home from handicraft." And before I could say more, my words were cut off by Barbara's voice. She whispered, "Girl he's standing over there."

My heart felt as if it had fallen into the bottom of a well. That well on my grandfather's property at "the Hill." My face felt hot. I was sure it had turned red. I secretly hoped that he would come over to where I stood because I didn't have the courage to turn and look at him. I admitted, "I can't look. What's he doing?" The other three gladly turned and gave Larry a firm stare, and Barbara slung her long hair as she turned to report, "He's coming this way!"

I felt my heart pound like the sound of a drumbeat, and suddenly, I heard Larry's voice. I looked up and he was standing in front of me.

He spoke to me and asked, "Hey, Emily, do you want to go over to the Hershey's Grill after school today?" He glanced over at the other girls who were standing nearby seemingly spellbound by this moment in time.

Taking in the essence of his appearance—his yellow skin, his warm and half-cracked smile that barely showed the rims of his teeth as he opened his mouth to speak—his eyes that lit up as he spoke to me, I hung onto his every word as I looked at him.

I knew I was glowing. I answered, "Sure. Where do you want to meet?"

"I think school is out at one today. I'll meet you right here at one--okay."

The two of us stood smiling at each other, and neither of us heard the school bell ring.

Barbara rushed over to me, grabbing my shoulder with her hand. "Come on here girl!" With our good-byes, we hurried away.

As I walked away at the insistence of Barbara, I turned quickly to give Larry an over the shoulder glance, but he had already walked away and disappeared into the crowd. "Shoot, he's gone," I groaned.

We four girls made our way through the crowded hallway to our assigned room with the stares of the other classmates upon us. Finding four desks we sat down looking about the room while waiting for the teacher to call the role.

I was pleased with the attention I had received from the classmates. I noticed that Hal Johnson and Robert from last year were going to be in the same room with me again this year.

Our ninth grade teacher stood in front of the room and asked everyone to be quiet. "I'm Mrs. Smith, and I want to welcome you to Westchester high school. I want to give you your permanent seats as I call the role."

She began calling the names of the students and the seating arrangements. Finally, she said, "Barbara Jones and Emily Jones." The two of us rushed across the room relieved to know we would have seats in the rows with Mildred and Silva, we quickly sat down. Mrs. Smith began writing an assignment for the class on the chalkboard. And before she could finish the work, I looked up because I heard the voice of someone calling my name.

"Emily, Emily." Larry was standing in the hallway by the door of my classroom. "I'll wait here for you."

I nodded my head up and down to let Larry know I had heard him.

At one o'clock, the school bell rang. I gave a quick glance out into the hallway to assure myself that Larry was still waiting there. He stood there with one arm propped against the wall, and one leg crossed the other. I left the classroom to make my way to where he stood. Before leaving the building, I waved good-bye to Barbara, but hoped that we would see each other later at the Grill.

Barbara's boyfriend, Sean, who was Silver brother, ran up to the classroom. With his arms around their necks he brought Barbara and Silver with him. Mildred said she needed to go home. Using one hand, he motioned to Larry to join them. The five of us walked out of the school building together, across the yard and down the walk to the grill.

Hershey's Grill was the center of the action for the young and the old Blacks in the fifties. It was right in the square in Bright Town and next door to the Blue Light Club. It was a dingy little room with a two-by-four kitchen that made the most delicious, greasy hamburgers in town. They were especially good with a Coke in the bottle. The aroma of fried chicken and hamburgers could be smelled a block away. The school kids would pack in the place after school like sardines in a can.

Hersey, the owner of the place was a big, fat, dark skinned, round-headed man with a belly like a wash pot. He was as greasy as his hamburgers, and he wore an apron tied around his belly that revealed his line of work—spots of ketchup, mustard and grease spatters. When he was cooking hamburgers, he would start sweating, and slapping the meat on the grill, and sucking on a bottle of Coke, and stirring the cabbage slaw with his chubby, black hands, and man, you knew there was going to be some good eating.

We walked into the grill, and found an empty booth where we sat near a narrow window. Larry and I sat on one side, Silver, Sean and Barbara on the other.

"You want a hamburger, Emily?" Larry leaned over and pulled his face near me. I gave a slight nod of affirmation with what I'm sure was a timid look in my eyes. I wasn't accustomed to socializing in this manner. I had never gone to the grill before. No boy had ever bought me a burger before. I thought--this is my very first date.

Larry got up to order saying before he left, "Come on man."

Sean rose to follow him. But before he left, he asked, "What-chall-want?"

Barbara took Sean by the hand smiled at him and said, "I want a hamburger, fries with ketchup and a Coke."

Silver smiling wider than Barbara said to Sean, "Me too."

Sean walked away with his hands in his pockets rattling the coins within and shaking his head, and the girls giggling.

Window fans blew in cool air across the room as the music blasted out "I'm Walking," By Fats Domino. Some couples were dancing on the hardwood floor- their skirt tails flying and shoulders shaking. Soon the pace was changed with a slow-dance record—"Earth Angel."

Larry made his way across the floor over to the booth where we girls sat and leaned in close to me. "Let's dance, Emily." I joined him on the dance floor as he encircled me in his arms, as we moved across the floor.

Before long, Larry felt a shove and it was Barbara's hand he felt, and I heard her voice command, "Open your eyes, boy!"

He simply turned his head and smiled at Barbara. Afterwards he put his mouth close to my ear and whispered, "Can I call you tonight?" As he continued to slowly turn me around on the floor.

I held on to him and responded without hesitation, "I don't have a telephone, but I can give you my grandmother's number. She lives next door."

"Will she get you when I call?"

"Uh huh, yea she will." I answered.

The music stopped, and the shuffling of feet across the wooden floor was heard as we made our way back to our booths. Larry walked me back to the booth where Silver sat alone.

"I'm going to check on our food. I'll be right back." He walked away and left me sitting with Silver. Barbara made her way back to the booth and joined the two of us.

Barbara looking around the room asked, "Where'd Sean go?"

Silver glanced around the room and answered, "There he is over there dancing with Susan."

Barbara poked out her mouth as if to pout. "I don't like her. She likes Sean." She could be such a baby about some things sometimes. And she really knew how to make her voice whine. "I wish he wouldn't dance with her especially when I'm looking right at him do it. Anyway he is supposed to be getting our food—not over there dancing with some other girl."

In an attempt to make Barbara feel better, "But look at who has him." She grabbed Barbara's hand and held it for a while. In an endeavor to change the subject, Silver questioned, "The tenth graders are having a dance on Friday after school at the Center. Do you want to go?"

And before Barbara has a chance to answer Sean had returned with the hamburgers and Cokes. He placed them in front of the girls. He asked, "Where's Larry?" keeping his eyes on Barbara with a devious looking grin on his mouth.

Barbara rolled her eyes at him but did not speak. "I'm going to find him."

"You make me sick, punk. You know you just want to get over there with Susan Thompson," exclaimed Barbara.

Sean looked at her in surprise. He began to walk away and glanced back at her once, puts his hands in his pockets rattling the coins again as he had before.

The three of us were silent and Silver and Barbara started to eat. Silver asked, "Now where's Larry?" Before anyone could answer, she continued, "Does he still try to talk to Beverly? You know they use to be real crazy about each other."

I didn't answer, but looked up at Silver.

"Heard that the only reason he was going with her was because she was 'easy'," chided Silver, "but she doesn't look as good as you do." She looked firmly at me, and she smiled widely. "We have eyes alike. Don't we Emily?"

I avoided starring back at her and answered reluctantly, "Ah yea, we do." But in my mind, I felt pity for Silver's attempt to identify with me. I felt the only comparison was that we were females. I wanted genuinely to say something encouraging, but I didn't for fear that it would be a lie. I could not give Silver the approving eye she desired.

Silver was the oldest of three, and she was supposed to be a sophomore. Her rationalization for repeating her freshman year in school was that "she was sure the teacher didn't like her since she wore clothes just as *good* as her teacher." Silver, Sean and their youngest brother were the only children in a single-parent family; whereupon, they were being brought up by the father in a one-bedroom house across the tracks in that part of town referred to as Bottle Neck. It was considered one of the roughest parts of the city where people in town said you wouldn't want to be caught there after dark because there was a lot going on.

Silver was a tall, skinny girl with dark skin and short hair, which she straightened with Madam Walker's Royal Crown hair grease. Most of the girls used Royal Crown. But Silver must have used it on her legs too because they were as greasy as her hair. She chewed on her hamburger while talking.

"Have you ever put a weenie up in you? Me and my cousin Nan tried it with a weenie one time."

Barbara began laughing wildly the kind that came from the center of her stomach. She had a mouthful of hamburger and covered her mouth so that she would not spray her food on Emily when she burst out laughing. The laugh dissolved momentarily, and she uncovered her mouth, asking, "How'd it feel?" She began laughing again.

"Shit, I couldn't get it in." Silver admitted. "I pushed the 'thang' and pushed it but it wouldn't go in."

Barbara started to cough; she picked up the bottle of Coke took a swallow and gulped it down. This time closing her eyes and laughing harder she held onto her stomach with both hands.

I looked on in astonishment at the two.

The conversation died down, and we sat with wide smiles on our mouths when Larry and Sean returned. Larry sat down beside me, handed me a Coke and a burger and gave me a kiss on the cheek.

I looked at him briefly, and began to unwrap all sides of the paper from my sandwich; I examined it and took a bite. I chewed for a while and then sipped on the Coke.

"Is it good?" Larry asked.

Yes I replied, yes. I kept on chewing.

Larry slid over a little distance from me, and leaned his head against the back of the seat, took a cigarette and put it between his lips, struck a match and lit the cigarette, and blew out the match. He looked as if he were playing James Dean in "Rebel without a Cause." Larry was the epitome of the spoiled Black kid; his parents owned the only mortuary business in town that gave every respectable Black citizen the glory of going into the ground with dignity. His parents were deacons at Friendship Baptist Church; they attended routinely and headed important committees. And his mother sang on the choir with June Kannapolis while his father sat around in church predicting who his next client might be.

Larry was considered a prime catch at Westchester for any lucky girl. He was a musician and played the saxophone in one of the local rock and roll bands. It was said, he could have the girl of his choice- and that he did with gusto and as little modesty as possible. The grapevine said he had been kicked out of two private schools east of the Mississippi except for those that didn't admit colored folks. He gazed into my eyes and asked me about the dance that the tenth graders were sponsoring as a fundraiser. Mr. Bass, the high school principal had warned us, "No dances." But I couldn't see how anything could possibly go wrong. After all, I would ask my mother to chaperone.

****

Part III
High School Dance

*T*he dance was over at twelve midnight, and although my mother, Martha, had chaperoned the event, Thomas, my father, had picked Mama up from the dance early.

Larry and I were left alone. We left the center and walked out into the cool October air. Larry surrounded me with his arms, kissed me on the ear and the two of us started toward my street. We walked arm in arm into the schoolyard, which was isolated and silent. It was dark except for a dim light post in the middle of the schoolyard that gave a romantic glow to the night. The moon was a big orange ball in the black ocean universe.

Larry took the cigarette he puffed on from his lips and put it out with his foot on the ground. Drawing me close to him, he kissed me. Then he led me to the school steps and braced my back against the school wall, and kissed me again. I freed myself then gazed at him saying, "I have to go home now. My mama will be looking for me." But deep inside I ached for his love. The echo of my mother's voice rang in my ear. The words of my mother were louder than the calling desire for Larry. They rang like the sound of a school bell— "Sex is a sin." She said, "But it's the best feeling in the world." I knew how I felt when Larry was near me holding me, and I was afraid—afraid of sex—of everything--afraid of losing Larry if I did not give in to him—to what I knew he wanted. I knew that my friends were "doing it." They had told me so.

****

The car pulled up in front of the house and I could hear the horn honk from inside. My heart pounded as I thought of being with Larry. I had thought about it half the night. I had lain in my bed dreaming of being his girl and of us together gliding around town in the back seat of Sean's car laughing, whispering to each other, all while listening to beautiful music. He had asked me to meet him after we left the school dance.

He had been gazing at me with intense curiosity like a young child observing a new toy through a clear store window. For a time he had not spoken, then he leaned forward to whisper in my ear, "Do you want to go riding with me tomorrow night?

His attention had meant everything. He wanted to spend his time with me. I observed the idea with such fascination. I felt myself blushing what must have been a bright red, and then I looked at him bashfully. He could have possibly asked the question for my consideration because he knew I was so young and had never had a boyfriend before. "Yes," I replied almost in a whisper as if I was afraid he might withdraw his request.

"Sean and I will pick you up at eight then." He said and grabbed both of my shoulders with his hands drawing me close to him. I knew he was admiring me, yet laughing at my naiveté. Then he did laugh out loud.

****

I wanted to be ready to go exactly at eight. I had arranged with Mama to get out of the house by telling her I belonged to a singing group, and was to attend an evening practice. I knew it was a lie, but I supposed all young girls tell lies when we wanted things to go our way. Mama had given her consent, saying, "You be back here before your Daddy gets home from work." Daddy had taken a second job to make ends meet. He wouldn't be home until midnight.

I glanced into the mirror at myself once and smiled because I was happy. I opened the door and ran outside to the car, thinking to myself—maybe it won't be too bad.

I wore a fitted brown skirt and white wool, pullover sweater with white socks. I hadn't had time to heat water and bathe the morning before, and I was concerned about myself. I smelled funky. But still, I rushed to the car. Larry opened the door, and I jumped in beside him, and into his arms.

The car started down the street with the two couples; Sean the driver and Barbara sat in the front seat with Larry and me in the back. We pulled up into a dark and isolated church yard and Sean stopped the motor of the car and turned off the lights leaving us in total darkness. We sat quietly for a moment. Sean broke the silence first. "I think I saw a ghost, Barbara."

"Where?" Don't say that, you know I'm scared of ghosts." We all laugh. Larry remains quiet with his eyes fixed on me.

"Sean, let's walk over there by that big tree," Barbara begged.

The two of them got out of the car and faded into the darkness.

Now being alone with me, Larry turned, and in his soft voice he said, "I love you Emily." He began to kiss me and lay me down on the car seat. I squirmed and Larry controlled me with his embrace. Now his kisses began to have more pressure against my mouth.

I whispered, "No Larry, I'm scared." Panting all the while, "I'm scared!"

"I told you," he whispered, "It will be all right so don't be afraid." He kissed me more, now with wet kisses causing a stream of sensations in me that made me feel more powerful, yet weaker at the same time.

Somehow the power I felt forced the words I was thinking to come to the surface, and I whispered in between his kisses, "I might get pregnant."

"You won't get pregnant. Don't worry." He stopped kissing me again and looked at me lying there. I felt small and fragile.

"If you do, I'll marry you." He whispered in my ear.

I felt the power of his body next to me, and then pointing down inside me, like the force of some object breaking open the water. I groaned with the pain, and all the while I felt the pleasurable sensation of his body next to, and on top of mine. Then I wanted him to stop, but any power I had faded away--I couldn't force him to stop. I wasn't sure if I really wanted him to stop. His body began to thrust in a motion that was unfamiliar, and I felt the earth move from under me like the ripple of an earthquake. I held on to Larry as though our bodies became one. We moved together now and in a few moments it was as if a volcano had erupted in him. We lay quietly as one. I lay there beside him with his arms wrapped around me feeling weak and helpless. I wasn't thinking of anything except that I felt his love for me and that it felt good to have it.

Larry, after a while, pulled himself up and watched me lying there. He leaned down and pulled my hair aside from my forehead and then placed a kiss there and then one on my mouth, my nose, my cheeks, my chin and both of my hands. And in a while I managed to sit up too, a little self-conscious at the way Larry kept his eyes fixed upon me.

"Things will be different between us now— you're my girl."

The words flowed from his mouth like honey from a tree when the sap is ripe, and I fell upon his lips to kiss the sweet taste that flowed when he spoke. I loved him. I would be his girl—he had said so. The two of us sat with great gentleness and privacy in each other's arms when Sean and Barbara returned.

"This car smells awful!" Sean blurted out sarcastically as he climbed into the car under the steering wheel and started the motor. Before he began to pull the car out of the churchyard and onto the road, he turned around in the seat and gazed at Larry trying all the while not to laugh.

Barbara was not joining in with Sean's chitchat, questioned, "What y'all been doing in here? She turns an eyed me. I remained silent.

Larry returned, "I'd like to smell where you've been."

Sean lets out a belly laugh that caused him to giggle with his whole body in the car seat, "Whatcha mean man?" as he allowed his laughter to subside to give his attention to his driving.

Larry retorts, "You know what I mean." And they both laugh.

"Y'all want to ride around some? Sean asks as he backs the car out of the church yard and onto the road.

Larry answered, "Yeah, gimme a cigarette man." Sean held his hand over his head to give Larry a cigarette and returned it to the wheel.

****

For some reason I couldn't eat my breakfast grits. I felt different but wasn't sure of the reason. I stood in the bathroom with the door partly cracked, and when I glanced up, my mother stood gazing at me.

"Did you start yet?"

It was as if Mama could read my mind. I felt the ice in my guts. I held my head low and answered dreadfully, "No I didn't."

Mama sucked in a deep breath through her nostrils, but didn't hesitate asking. "Have you and Larry been messing around!?"

I stiffened to keep my voice from shaking. I had tiptoed around the house and around Mama for several days hoping not to draw any attention upon myself ever since my "date" with Larry. I hoped that I wouldn't have to answer this particular question-- not now--not today—not ever, and now I had no choice--I had to, now that Mama had asked. I started to shake almost as if I would fall apart. The dread I felt about Mama's question was real. I felt the ice in my throat this time it froze my speech for a time.

Mama demanded, "Answer me girl!"

Finally, after some time had passed as the two of us stood, "Yeah," I almost whispered it. And in doing so, my body began to shake again—I felt cold and then hot--I thought I would surely faint.

"You mean to tell me you have been doing something with Larry after I warned you about it?" I felt the ice again.

The ice symbolized the void of information that I supposed Mama thought I knew. But I didn't know. I could not know what she neglected to tell me. I remembered her saying something about doing things against the Holy word, but she failed to explain what that meant. She failed to show me the scripture from the Bible to help me remember. How could I remember when she herself had said—"it's the best feeling in the world." I know she said that because it was when I *started*.

Mama walked away from the door and began to hum an old church song, "Like a Bridge Over Troubled Waters." She walked to the bed and, and there she sat down and placed her hands on her thighs. She kept humming her song. She was in deep thought— somewhere far away it seemed.

When I came from the bathroom, I saw Mama sitting there on the bed. Fixing her eyes on me, she commanded, "Come over here girl." I didn't change my stride, and walked in Mama's direction.

"Lay down here." Mama directed.

I lay down on the bed beside Mama; I felt small lying there and afraid. Mama took her hands and began to feel the outline of my stomach. It was the first time I had seen Mama look old and weary. When she stopped the two of us were silent.

I sat up beside Mama. She laid her head in her hand, "Lord, Lord, Lord. When I was seventeen," Mama began, "I got wid your sister, and me and your daddy married, and then I got wid you. We were living over there on Seaboard Street and before you were born; your daddy was drafted off in the Army and sent overseas." She continued, "He didn't think he was gonna get to see you, 'cause he didn't know whether he would live or die over there fighting in World War II. Huh, huh, huh, sometime we didn't have nothing wid all you chaps." She looked at me now, "What in the world do you wanna get with a baby for? Ain't even finished high school yet." She questioned, "Will Larry marry you?"

I stared into Mama's eyes, and into the depth of her soul. It seemed that I touched the essence of my mother's life with my eyes. I remained silent to Mama's question. With my mind's eye, I saw the answer, but as a lamb, I feared the tiger. I remembered Larry's words. They flashed through my brain like a streak of lightening through a dark cloud during a storm. Still I did not answer.

"Does he know you're pregnant?" She asked.

"He knows I didn't come on my period." I held my head low as I said this. When I said it, it didn't make me unhappy. In my heart, I wanted to have it, and it didn't make me unhappy. In my heart I wanted to have Larry's baby, and to be the mother of his child— his wife. As I sat there, I thought all this and more.

I thought about how different my life would be, with Larry over there in the big house where he lived, sleeping between the clean white sheets, and in the comfortable bed. I recalled the smell that came from his kitchen like sweet bread, and the pale blue curtains which covered the big picture window. I remembered the stillness of his living room. It looked like some picture book magazine, as if nobody ever used it. It was clean like the smell of those downtown furniture stores that you walk in sometimes to look around at all the pretty things.

There wouldn't be any children running and messing all over the place there. There would be lots of good food to eat. This is what I wanted. After all, Larry loved me and I loved him.

Mama broke the silence when she rose from the bed. Before she left, she affectionately slapped me on the shoulder lightly with her hand.

****

When the telephone rang, I was sitting on the sofa at Grandma AJ's house waiting for the call. I picked up the receiver.

Larry's voice said, "Emily."

I answered, "Yeah?"

Larry continued, "My mother said you called."

"Yeah, I did."

"Larry, my mother asked me if you knew that I am pregnant."

For a few moments I heard Larry breathing. He then spoke. "What else did she say?"

"She wanted to know if you would marry me."

When I said this, it was almost as if I was asking too—to reassure myself.

Larry answered me in an assuring tone. "Emily you know I will. Did you tell her that?"

I answered him softly, "Yeah, I did." In my mind I knew I wanted to tell Mama that Larry would marry me.

****

I fluffed the pillows on the sofa and straightened the purple cloth covering. Knowing that Larry would be coming at eight, I wanted to feed the kids and clean the house before his arrival. The sizzling sound which came from the kitchen caught my ear, and dropping the broom, I rushed in, snatched up the lid on the pan, and turned the potatoes that fried in the hot grease on the stove. Replacing the lid on the pan, I turned and noticed my little sister, Rosie, standing beside me sucking her thumb. "Gimme some tatoes, Emily," Rosie begged. She took her thumb out of her mouth and held her hand up to me.

I smiled at Rosie and pulled the oven door open. I picked out a round, browned potato and handed it to my little sister.

"Now go play in there while I clean up. I'll feed you in a minute." At that moment, Jimmy and Greg rushed up to me. "We want some," the boys begged together.

Greg pulled the oven door open before I can stop him and peeked in. He grabbed a handful of potatoes and ran away, and Jimmy chased after him. Jimmy caught up with Greg and pulled him to the floor. The two scuffle as Greg stuffed the potatoes into his mouth. "I told you to gimme some. I'm gonna tell Mama that you took her quarter off the dresser."

Greg stared at Jimmy, poked out his mouth and insists, "I didn't."

I get between my two brothers. "Get in there Greg. You too Jimmy!" Both of you are too big to be acting like this. Now stop it!

> Jimmy ran to the back of the house saying, "I'm
> gonna tell Mama. I gonna tell Mama!"

Jimmy ran to the back of the house saying, "I'm gonna tell Mama. I gonna tell Mama! Greg ran away too.

■■

I picked up the broom and continued sweeping he dim linoleum rug which covered the floor. I prepared the table and my sisters and brothers were beaconed to their meals. The children rushed to the table and jumped onto their chairs with watering mouths.

■■

Rationing out their portions, I left the best portions and parts for the older folks who were away at work, and who would be coming home with empty stomachs. I did not join my siblings because I was too busy and tense to eat.

The children had not completed their meals before the knock was heard at the door. I jumped inside to think that it was Larry. I peeked through the curtain and he stood there waiting for me to open the door.

The aroma of fried potatoes, fried bologna, biscuits and collard greens came out to hit Larry, as I opened the door to receive him.

"Did you cook dinner?" He asked as he walked over to the sofa and sat down.

I answered, "Yeah."

"Don't you want some water or some tea?"

He answered seeming uneasy, "I don't think so."

Turning to me, he kissed me on the lips. "What did you cook," He asked with that half grin on his mouth I loved so much to see.

I started calling off the menu, fried potatoes, green, biscuits…, and Larry interrupted.

"Tell me what your mama said when she found out."

I felt nervous, a little startled when I answered, "She wanted to know if…if you would marry me."

"Does your father know?"

"I don't think so."

Larry had been sitting on the edge of the sofa at first when we began talking. He fell back as if the wind had been knocked out of him when he heard this. He sat there for a moment, then stood up and walked to the door, staring at the window. Turning, he squarely looked at me and asked me, "Do you want to get married Emily?" He kept his eyes fixed on me.

I answered without any hesitation, "Yes!"

Larry walked back to where I sat and placed his body beside mine. Before he could tell me that's what we would do, a voice called me from the kitchen. It was Rosie wanting tea. I immediately went to my sister's aid.

When I returned to Larry's side, he said his mind was on the previous day when he had told his parents about the pregnancy. He began to tell me, "They were in the den after dinner watching television." He said, "I remember it so clearly. Over and over" he said, "I could hear my mother's words. You'll never be able to go to college now. You'll have to go to work to support your family. As she said this, she flopped her body down on the chair, her head was in her hands and she cried. She couldn't stand to see her baby boy suffer in such a way." Larry told me, he remembered his father standing there against the cabinet looking stern and gentlemanly as he spoke. "You'll have rent to pay, grocery bills, gas bills, and baby shoes to buy. Why, you'll work yourself to death!"

He said his mother had stopped crying. "She was not looking forward to the day when her only son—her only child would 'do such a thing." She did not want me to marry you Emily. She impressed upon my mind, "After this baby is born, how many more will there be?"

Larry told me, he remembered sitting there and not being able to fight against his parents and what they wanted for him. He said he excused himself from the room and walked into the back yard.

The silence there was louder than it had ever been, but he knew he could not go back inside. He started walking and found himself across town in the Bottle Neck at Sean's house. There he said he spent the night. It was the first time he had ever stayed away from home all night without telling his parents his whereabouts.

Afterward, Larry sat on the sofa seemingly in deep thought. His meditation was broken when my mother, Martha entered the living room door. She did not see him at first. A neighbor outside still held her attention. She said good-night to them and noticed Larry as she turned her head in his direction.

Mama usually arrived home from work from the white folks' house every evening about supper time, always exhausted. A few minutes later, Thomas came in after his wife. He picked her up every evening after work, would eat his dinner, and leave them there to go off to his second job. Thomas walked slowly, and anyone would know he had had a hard day by the subdued manner he spoke. "Hi y'all." He threw up his hand and managed a smile.

Mama smiled at Larry warmly, showing her white teeth against her ebony skin. She gave him a big, "Hey."

He returned, "Hi you'll doing?"

My parents disappeared into the bedroom.

As I sat on the sofa beside Larry, his words resounded in my mind, 'I don't think they want me to marry you Emily.' But I thought, but you promised—you promised! My mind ached, my heart ached too.

Soon, Ruth, the oldest was home too, and all the family was in. The house buzzed with the voices of the family. The little ones were running around playing, the older ones watching television, talking, holding one of the little ones on their lap and rocking him. It seemed Larry felt a part of all of this. His comfort seemed more at home here, than when he was with his own parents. It seemed, ironically that he felt like he really belonged here with me.

****

It was twelve midnight, and the house was quiet. I was holding my little sister, Rosie, on my lap. I had rocked her to sleep. Larry still sat beside me.

Mama had retired after dinner and Daddy had retired after returning home from his second job to rest for the coming day.

I rose to put my sister to bed and in doing so, the girl awakened. Rocking her a little as I walked through the room where my mother and father slept, I placed Rosie in bed beside her sister Brenda. I covered her with a blanket and left her there.

When I passed Mama's bed, she turned over and raised her head to see who was passing. Upon seeing it was me, she said, "Emily, it's time for you to go to bed now." She then turned over and lay down again.

"Okay Mama."

Larry must have heard Mama's words; when I returned to the living room, he was standing at the front door. We went outside to the front porch. We kissed each other good-bye standing on the porch step.

"I'll call you tomorrow Emily, before I come over. I love you." He tightly held me in his arms as he said these words.

I returned, "I love you too, Larry." I watched him turn and walk away—away from my house—away from the porch—away from my life for a long, long time.

Part IV
Discoveries

*T*he crowd roared when the hitter slammed the ball across the field for a home run. I sat on my neighbor Cen's porch watching from a distance. I thought about Larry and felt that I would perhaps see him at the game. I wore a tight-fitted skirt with a sleeveless blouse tied in front, and sandals. I wanted to look radiant sitting there hoping to see Larry. Cen a girl a year younger than me sat with me. We had been friends for a long time. We sometimes attended the movies and visited each other, or sometimes we just sat around on the porch and talked. "Let's walk down to the field so we can see better," Cen begged in a carefree manner. She rose and began to descend the steps. As I stood, a passing car stopped and backed up to where we stood.

"Can I go with you—you in the tight skirt? The driver yelled. "What's your name, Baby?" Realizing that they couldn't get my attention, they sped off with wheels screaming.

Marveling at the attention, we crossed the street slowly and found a seat on the benches, under all the lights, to watch the baseball game between Bent Hill and Westchester. The spirit of the crowd was high, and it seemed that everyone from New Town had turned out for the event. I looked around to see if I could spot

Barbara or Silver. Not seeing either of them, I settled back and decided they must have stayed at home. I sat watching the game, when a tall, brown-skinned young man obviously older approached and introduced himself.

"I'm Walter and you must be Larry's girl, Emily." He said.

"I'm a good friend of Larry's."

"I believe I have heard Larry mention your name." I said.

I watched as I saw Walter take his long legs and step over one seat and climbed up to sit beside me. He asked, "Do you mind if I sit beside you?"

"No, I don't mind."

Then Walter doesn't waste any time delivering the startling news. "Larry is gone to New York," he said and watching my reaction.

I felt a strong, strange feeling inside. I felt hot and cold all at once. My heart I'm sure skipped a beat before I spoke. When I did speak, I asked, "What do you mean?" I almost stuttered, "Go-gone where?"

"He left on a bus of bean pickers going to New York to pick beans." He said he was going to work there for the summer."

I felt the pain begin—first in my heart and then in my mind. He hadn't even come by or called to tell me his intentions. He hadn't said what he wanted me to do. Yet he had said he loved me and would marry me. I questioned, "Has it all been a lie?"

I fought desperately to hold back tears as I sat under Cen and Walter's eyes.

Walter didn't watch the game. His attention was consumed by my presents. In a short while, "Would you like for me to walk you home when the game is over?" He asked in a soft, kindhearted expression.

I sat there for a moment before answering. I wanted so much for what he said to be untrue. I sat there hoping that at any moment Larry would appear and things would be right. "God please don't let it be true," was all I could think. I repeated this prayer over and over in my mind.

Walter apparently wasn't sure I had heard him, and he repeated his question. "Do you want me to, ah, walk you home after the game?"

Coming out of my daze, I said to him, "Yea, I think I want to leave now."

Cen, while listening to Walter and me revealed a bewildered expression on her face for what she heard. Yet she did not interrupt; she only listened.

I turned to her, "Cen, I think I'll go home now. Are you going to stay?"

"No, I think I'll go home too." "Emily," she asked with obvious concern, "You didn't know Larry was leaving?"

I dreaded her question. It cut through my heart like the sharp blade of a knife. How could I bring myself to face so many questions—to tell the truth? I felt my heart sink. I wanted to scream and let the tears flow. I fought hard to maintain control. "No, I didn't know he had gone." I said to Cen. The three of us rose and nobody spoke until we were on the street in front of the baseball diamond and Cen's house.

"I'll talk to you tomorrow, Cen."

"Bye Emily. See you Walter." Cen was heard as she ascended the steps of her front porch.

It wasn't a good feeling to walk home not knowing whether I may have lost Larry forever. I felt so bewildered and lonely. What was I going to do was the question.

We walked in the direction of home, and Walter began. "Larry told me that you are pregnant."

Now I felt absolutely alone, betrayed and embarrassed. I did not speak.

Walter continued, "I don't think he wants to marry you." We approached the step of my porch. "Will you stay here and talk to me for a little while?" He requested.

Without answering, I mechanically stopped and sat down on the porch. Walter sat beside me. We both sat staring out into space seemingly at nothing, perhaps both thinking of this moment—I thought of my predicament—and now looking back retrospectively, I know Walter's thoughts were probably about his unpredicted opportunity. Not for a moment did he think of Larry and me staying together, in spite of the fact that he had gone to New York only for the summer. He wanted the triumph of taking his best friend *Larry's girl* behind his back—one of the girls he probably felt was too beautiful for his conquest all by himself.

Some moments of time passed, when Walter said, "You are so beautiful. And if Larry won't marry you, then I will." He kept his eyes on me as to admire the beauty he had just spoken of. He continued, "Your long black hair hanging around your soft shoulders, your tan skin shining in the moonlight; your dark eyes, small nose and mouth are so, so beautiful. I wish I could take you in my arms at this moment, hold you close to me—console you, make you know that I care so much for you. Just the sight of you makes me love you. To me, you are just a baby yourself, so small, so innocent. I had not known you before." He sighed. "I had only seen you occasionally in passing—with Larry. I never in my wildest dreams, thought that one day I would be sitting beside you like this. You had been Larry's girl." Walter places his arm around my shoulder; he wanted a girl that possessed the pretty but innocent demeanor that moved him to go the limits even if it meant marriage, even if it was perhaps a cruel intention. His interactions and experiences as a college boy at the university taught him how to manipulate the naïve. He asks, "Can I come and see you tomorrow?"

I stood, and his arm fell away. "I don't think so; I have a lot to do tomorrow."

Walter rose and walked away leaving me standing here. "Good night, Walter." I thought of him for a brief moment, and I turned to go inside the house.

The house was quiet. It was summer and I fell crying onto my bed. As I cried, all the heavens must have felt my sorrows. I wept for the very life that I carried inside me—the life that Larry and I had made from love. Now I was abandoned.

****

I lay sobbing in bed when I felt Mama's hands picking me up into her arms and holding me. Wiping my tears away, Mama said, "Don't cry Baby. It will be all right."

When Daddy heard the commotion, he appeared at the door of my room. "What's the matter with her?"

"Nothing, she'll be all right." Mama turned and gave him a look that meant go back to bed. And he did.

Everyone had by now retired and I lay in bed trying to sleep. But in the adjourning room, Thomas and Martha lay awake. "What's the matter with Emily, Martha? He turns to face her in bed.

Martha hesitated, sighed and said, "Thomas, now don't get mad, but Emily's pregnant.

Thomas was stunned when he heard the news. "What? Well, good Lord! How in the world did that happen? Martha, you know it's Larry's he's the only boy that's been hanging around here. I knew he's been hanging around here too much, damn it!" There is silence. Then, "Well, what's she gonna do?"

"Thomas, I don't know now."

"Has Larry said anything about it?"

"Naw, I haven't talked to him. I just found out the other day myself. So I don't know what he's planning to do. But I know he's gonna have to do something."

"How in the world they gonna take care of a baby – both of them as young as they are? That scoundrel might not even marry her."

Martha sighed, "Thomas, I just don't know."

****

When morning came, the family was gathered around the wood table which sat in the middle of the kitchen floor. Thomas sat with a concerned look on his face. Martha knew why. He did not speak but remained silent.

Mama spoke first. Emily, *do* Larry know you're pregnant?

"Yeah Mama, he knows."

"Well, what are you gonna do? Will the two of you get married or what?"

I sat there for a moment and thought of Larry and that he was gone. I wanted to say the words, but somehow they became heavy in my throat. Forcing my vocal cords to vibrate, I said painfully, "Larry is gone to New York, Mama. He left last week on a bean truck." The tears filled my eyes. My words made Thomas furious.

"What the hell did he go off to New York for, knowing you gone have a baby? That sure as hell was a stupid thang to do. Look like to me if he cared anything 'bout you, he would have stayed right here and married you."

Mama turned to me, "Emily, do you want to do anything about the pregnancy?"

I felt afraid—I felt a horrible fear overtake my body. The idea that my mother could ask such a thing— DO ANYTHING ABOUT THE PREGNANCY! I loved Larry and wanted his child.

****

It was midnight and the rain beat down on the roof of the house; I lay in my bed listening attentively, and thinking of what had transpired during the morning. I climbed out of bed and walked to the kitchen for a glass of water. Taking a glass from the dish rack, I ran the faucet for a short while, until the water felt cool to my hand. Suddenly as I glanced outside the kitchen window I was startled when I noticed a tall figure standing there. I stared for a moment trying to make out the figure. Then I could see that it was Walter standing there in the rain. "My Lord, that's Walter." I said to myself. "What's he doing standing there in the rain?" I turned off the water and rushed to the kitchen door, opened it and went outside onto the porch. "Walter, is that you?" I called to him.

Walter stood there as if in a daze. He did not answer. I called to him again realizing he had not heard me. "Walter is that you? Now hearing me and being brought out of his daze, he turned his head mechanically in my direction.

At first it seemed that he did not see me. I supposed that I was swallowed by the darkness. And when he did see me, he walked over to the porch where I stood and spoke in a soft whisper.

"Oh, how you doing Emily?" He asked. And before I could respond, he continued. "I guess you're surprised to see me standing here at this time of night." He let out a little sad chuckle.

I answered him, "Yeah, I am." The two of us stood there, me on the porch, and him below me on the ground, with the rain falling.

Walter began again, "I didn't mean for anybody to catch me standing here, but, I guess the time just slipped by as I started to think about you. I was just passing by on my way home from down the street and well, here I am." He laughed his little laugh again.

I began to feel flattered and pity at the same time by the thought that Walter would stand outside my window in the rain thinking of me. I began to ask myself: Does he really love me? Will he marry me like he said and be the father of my baby? The thought of it all made me smile. So now I stood smiling at him. The two of us stood smiling at each other now, under the hidden moon, and the hidden stars, in the rain, in the middle of the night.

Walter took a step forward and the next thing I knew, he stood close to me on the porch. He touched my cheek with his hand. "You're so beautiful." He said.

We stood gazing into each other's eyes. He leaned down, and was about to kiss me when the light in the kitchen came on. Mama stood at the door. "Emily, what are you doin' out there in the rain? Come in this house right now!" She commanded angrily.

Walter and I were both startled by Mama's voice, and Walter rushed away without saying good-bye, and I scurried into the house.

"Who was that?" Mama asked.

I answered her with caution, "It was Walter Phifer. I got up to get some water, and when I looked outside, he was standing there looking at the house." I tried to explain.

"In the rain?—Standing out there like that this time of night? You-go-to-bed!" Martha turned to return to her bed beside Thomas, and I trailed along behind her.

Soon the house was quiet again, and all during the night I found it hard to sleep. The thought that Walter loved me kept surfacing in my mind. I asked myself a million times whether I would marry him— whether my parents would approve—whether Larry would come back for me—what would he think of my marrying his best friend. Finally, sleep drifted into my heart and into my soul.

> Oh sleep!
> It is a gentle thing,
> Beloved from pole to pole!
> To Mary Queen the praise be
>   Given!
> She sent the gentle sleep
>   From Heaven, that
> Slide into my soul.
>   Samuel Taylor Coleridge
>   **The Rhyme of the**
>   **Ancient Mariner**

****

My hands shook when I opened the envelope. It was a letter postmarked from New York—it was from Larry. I took a deep breath and started to read the lines. But it wasn't what I hoped to read:

EMILY, WHAT'S THE IDEA OF YOU LETTING WALTER COME TO SEE YOU? NO DECENT GIRL MESSES AROUND WITH MORE THAN ONE MAN. ONLY WHORES DO THINGS LIKE THAT. ANYWAY, WALTER WAS SUPPOSED TO BE MY FRIEND. HA HA! SOME BEST FRIEND....Larry.

I didn't see or hear from Larry again. When I began to "show," Walter and I were soon married.

Dr. Clegg did deliver my baby in January; and immediately after Raven was born, he cut the umbilical cord, then he leaned down and placed a kiss on my forehead, "You're the best patient I've ever had." He said. As I think about it now, it didn't dawn upon me then, but now though, I believe he was taking his opportunity to "seal with a kiss" the secret of his molestation of me. Perhaps what I had not told before now was never to be spoken—I didn't know just how helpless I was.

****

I thought I had died and gone to heaven when Walter's parents learned through "the grapevine", June Kannapolis, and Mae Raleigh made a special trip to the Macums funeral home to deliver the news of our marriage, and Walter's whole family, his mother, father and two sisters made the rare visit to our house to see me shortly afterwards, and Mrs. Phifer's oldest daughter, Lizzie, told me later what her mother said about me, "She's as pretty as a doll." When Raven was a month old, Walter and I moved into the house with his parents.

****

It was Saturday night, and the Green Spot, a neighborhood club right down the hill from Walter's parent's house, was filled with the stench of fried food, fried hair, and the sweaty thick of the crowd on the dance floor. The red lights were dim, and the couples danced across the floor. When Walter went out at night, he preferred to take me along. Being a child, I didn't know any better than to tag along, whether it was safe or not. So at the Green Spot, Walter sat with me at the bar—he drank a beer. Walter was serious about his weekend play—getting dressed up and going out to juke joints to drink—whether I was able to go or not—he was going! Before he married me, he had been a college student at Johnson C. Smith University in the queen city until the summer we met; he had already decided he wasn't going to return to school. So he had many clothes—colorful shirts, pants and matching jackets— that collegian- look. "You're Mine", a popular blues song by Ritchie Valens began to play on the juke- box, and Walter asked me to dance. We walked to the middle of the crowd of other dancers and started to glide around on the floor. Walter looked up and seemed surprised to noticed Larry standing at the end of the bar. I don't believe he knew the man he had so easily betrayed—this so called best friend was back in Morristown. He had made an all out effort to warn Larry's parents Mr. and

Mrs. Macums that if he as much as heard of him in our vicinity, Larry would have hell to pay. He would kill him.

Immediately Larry's attention became apparently noticeable. He was looking in our direction. For some reason or another, Walter could not allow sleeping dogs to lie. He intentionally danced us over to where Larry stood and offered my hand to Larry. "You want to dance with her?" He asked with an obvious overly pleasant tone.

Larry answered, "Yeah, sure." Seemingly, not knowing what he was supposed to do, not refusing for fear he might injure my feelings—hurt my pride. He reached for me and took me in his arms. I grasped the man that I loved; I held on to him tightly but trying not to be obvious—trying not to provoke Walter's anger because I knew he was watching intently.

As Larry danced he kept his eyes on me, then he whispered in my ear, "Emily, do you still love me?" That question stirred up emotions I had tried to bury deep in my mind that caused beads of perspiration to appear on my face, as I whispered back to him, "You know I love you so much, Larry.

"I love you too Emily." Larry responded.

Nothing else was said. I thought to myself, nothing else matters. Larry was satisfied just to know that I still love him, and therefore, nothing else matters—not the responsibility of his child, my unhappiness with Walter, my welfare as the mother of his child—nothing. How could I possibly be happy with Walter—loving *him?* He was satisfied that I loved him, but more than that he was removed from the situation—he was free. He had my love, but he was free. He floated around on the dance floor in such a carefree manner with all eyes seemingly upon us.

The two of us twirled in each other's arms. The music stopped, and Larry returned my hand to Walter. "Thank you." Larry said as he walked away to the other side of the bar. He ordered a drink.

When I returned to his side at the bar, Walter seem to sense that something had happened between Larry and me. He set his eyes on me, "What's wrong? What was he saying to you?"

I hesitated before speaking, "He said he loved me." I was young. How was I supposed to know what to say except that Larry had told me he loved me, and it had made me feel good?

The expression on Walter's face began to change. He sat the glass bottle down hard on the bar which he held in his hand and stalked with stiffness over to where Larry stood. His annoyance was apparent, everyone could hear him, "Larry, you think you can whip my ass?" He didn't care who listened.

Larry appeared stunned by the question, glanced over to where I sat before he answered. He said, "I never thought about it Walter."

"THINK ABOUT IT THEN! Why did you tell *my wife* that you still love her?" Still raising his voice.

Larry, seeming not to know what to expect, hesitated then he could be heard, answered revealing tension in his voice, "Because I do." The anxiety in his voice subsided—he leaned against the bar seemingly more relaxed than before his answer. He looked like he felt good. The half grin on his face so familiar to me said it all. The grin that said he didn't care about the consequences, now that he told Walter how he truly felt—his truth.

Walter looked at him with a look of hatred—his teeth clenched—lips pinched tightly together. He did not speak again, but instead, turned and walked away with his fist squeezed together and back to my side.

This again was the last time I saw Larry for a long, long time. I later discovered that Larry had no intentions of doing the right thing by me once he learned of the pregnancy and his parents told him, "This is going to ruin your whole life if you marry that girl." I learned that they told him, *those people* have a lot of babies." I suppose they were basing it on the evidence at hand. After all there were ten of us at the time. Mama later had another baby, making it eleven.

When Raven was ten months old, we made the trip to New York to start a new life.

****

Part V
New York

*T*he train pulled up at the station on a hot day in mid-July. The porter yelled, New York City!" Passengers bailed out and onto the pavement. I was among them. I carried my baby, Raven in my arms, and a diaper bag and purse in my hand. As I glanced around the crowd I heard my name called. "Emily!" Walter ran toward me. He ran to us and put his arms around Raven and me. He kissed first me then Raven. "Hey little pumpkin." He smiled a huge smile revealing his pleasure at the sight of us. "Do you want me to take the baby?" He asked.

"Yeah."

He took Raven in one arm and put the other around my shoulder again. "Come on, let's get your bags. I have a room in this lady's house in Jamaica, Long Island. It's nice. Don't have a TV, but I have a record player." He looked at me as we walked. "Girl, you look pretty."

I smiled back at him, "How did you come to the station?"

"A friend drove me."

We walked up to the baggage counter. "Where is your ticket?"

I reached into my purse and pulled out a yellow claim ticket. "Here it is." I said, handing it to the middle-aged, tall, black man, standing behind the counter. He took the ticket, examined the number, and turned to locate the bag. He ran his eyes up the rack, and then down, when he came to two brown cardboard suitcases; he took them from the rack.

"Here you go." He said.

Walter asked me to take the baby, and he grabbed my luggage. "This way," he said, as he gave a little jerk with his head in the direction we were to go. "We'll have to take the subway home." We crossed Nostrand Avenue and 43rd Street. I gazed around to the sights of black people, brown people, white people, large, small, short, and tall; they all walked as they didn't know anyone they encountered, not like the people in Morristown, where everyone threw up their hand and waved or said "Hey" as they passed. There was something else different too. They all seemed to be in some great hurry, and they didn't even look at you as they passed—keeping their eyes straight ahead in one direction. It seemed the only thing they thought of was where they might have been going.

When we left the subway station, we walked through the city to a brownish gray house on Long Island. Walter rang the bell, and a middle aged, dark skinned lady, wearing a nurse's dress opened the door.

"Hi Walter, oh my goodness this must be your little wife. Come on in." She said.

I entered and said hello as Walter introduced me. "This is Emily. Emily, this is Mrs. Randal.

"Did you have a nice trip?" She asked.

"Yeah, it was okay." I answered while looking around inspecting the place.

Holding out her arms, Mrs. Randal asked, "Can I hold the baby." She took Raven in her arms.

"She might be real wet." I said and began to inspect Raven's diaper.

"Why don't you change her?" I Withdrew Raven from her.

"I'll change her." I said taking Raven from Mrs. Randal.

Walter came in with the baggage and carried it upstairs. He yelled, "Come on up Emily."

I took a diaper from the bag which I carried, and changed Raven, and took her in my arms and went upstairs to where Walter stood in the doorway.

The room was small, but warm and dimly lighted. A bed dominated the middle of the floor, and faced a small radiator, which Walter had lined with a variety of candy bars, soft drinks, and a loaf of bread, bologna and a bottle of liquor. In one corner sat a record player atop a chest of drawers and a small window provided light, which was shaded with gray curtains.

I sat on the bed and held Raven in my arms. Walter came over and told me how much he had missed me. At that moment, there was a knock at the door, and the landlady stood there, and again the two of us parted for that moment.

"Come on in."

Mrs. Randal stepped into the room wearing a very wide grin. "Is everything okay?" She asked, looking over at Emily and then the baby.

Walter answered, "Everything is all right now that we're together; yeah, everything is just fine."

Mrs. Randal went over to where the baby lay on the bed and leaned over, "Oh look at you. Come here." She picked Raven up into her arms. She rocked her back and forth for a while, smiled at her and lay her down on the bed.

Walter went over to the chest of drawers and turned to Mrs. Randal. "Would you like to see this?" He handed her a small white book which I had constructed.

Mrs. Randal took the book, opened it and began to read from it: Although we are apart, I think of you often…She chuckled and made a remark about the way although was spelled. She said "A-l-t-h-o."

I was more than embarrassed, and angered at the same time. But I didn't make a fuss over what I had privately written that was for Walter and me only.

Before Mrs. Randal had a chance to read further, the telephone rang downstairs, and she excused herself to go and answer it.

The two of us were alone again, and Raven dry, warm and fed and lying on her stomach fell asleep.

Walter turned to me, "Do you like the place." He came close to me and took me in his arms—kissed me.

I was cold and hot with longing for Larry, but I forced myself to respond to Walter's passion. I smiled and said, "I like the way you fixed the place up."

Walter rose and went over to make himself a drink with some of the liquor and soda, which lined the radiator. I watched him fill his glass and drink it down in one huge gulp. He smacked his lips afterwards. He poured a second and drank it the same way he did the first. This time he wiped his mouth with the back of his hand.

He acted happy now and started to play some music on the small record player that sat on the chest of drawers.

I was only there metaphysically, and I was tired but I was not going to deny Walter, and besides I knew he was not going to allow me to.

He sat on the bed again and began to kiss me softly. He kissed me and in the mirror of my mind it was my love—the man I dreamed of had his lips on mine. And this was my life now--the memory of the first. The memory of his touch—his body scent—his essence. I longed for him and my mind ached that he was not here—here to know my love for him, to see our child. But this was my life now. I began to cry. I couldn't keep the tears from forming in my eyes. A tear trickled down my cheek, and Walter wiped it away.

"I know you don't love me, but I have enough love for both of us." He said. He seemed to know what I was thinking—what I was feeling. I believed he wanted desperately to mean every word for my sake and his. But inside I also knew he deeply despised the memory of Larry. He hated the shadow his memory cast over us. He held me and clinched his teeth. I heard his whisper, "Damn him!"

In a short while the three of us lay silent—Walter, the baby Raven and me.

****

The knock at the door awaken Raven, and she began to cry. Walter opened the door and Mrs. Randal stood there. She asked Walter to step outside.

She was heard, "Walter, I came for the rent; you said you would bring it down to me."

"Oh, ah, well, you see this guy is supposed to lend me some money today. I'll get it to you tonight." He said.

"But that's not what you said, Walter, I have to have the rent."

Walter became angry. His anger is aroused by the idea everything is being spoiled. He raised his voice,

"Look Old Woman, you'll get your damn money." He walked back into the room and slammed the door. "Mother fucker! God damn bitch! Emily, get up, get dressed! We're going over to a friend's house."

I was afraid, and I don't question what Walter is doing because I heard the conversation at the door. I dared not question him—not now in his anger. I dressed myself and readied Raven, while Walter made himself a bologna sandwich.

The three of us were stopped at the door by Mrs. Randal. "Walter when will you get the money? I have to have my rent or you'll have to get out."

"Old Woman, you'll get your damn money. Didn't I tell you that?" He had been eating his sandwich, and he stopped to tell her off; afterwards, he threw it down on the ground.

"You told me yesterday you would have the money today. I can put you out; you know you have not paid me in over three weeks!" Mrs. Randal snapped.

Walter goes into his pocket and comes out with a knife in his hand now. Mrs. Randal opens her mouth in amazement. I hold on tightly to Raven.

"Bitch, I'll cut your mother-fucking throat if you don't leave me alone!"

Mrs. Randal rushed inside and her voice is heard, "I'll call the police."

Walter grabbed me by the arm, "Come on!" Partly jerking, partly dragging me as he went. We hurriedly walked down the steps onto the sidewalk and out of sight of the house leaving our belonging except for Raven's diaper bag behind.

We walked down the street, and for a time, the silence which hung over our heads was dark as a cloud during a storm. I was as fearful as the fawn in the forest away from the protection of her mother deer.

The fear held me in a state which could be called shock. Shock of the reality which reminded me of Walter's other side. This was an unseen side which I hoped not to recognize in the man who had said he had enough love for both of us—the man who was supposed to protect Raven and me—he had promised.

The fright was felt throughout my frail body. The frail body with the small knot at the bottom of my stomach that revealed I now carried *Walter's child.* I clung tightly to the bundle I carried in my arms as if the baby was still there in my womb too. The little body gave me some kind of warmth and security that I wasn't getting from Walter.

As Walter stepped hurriedly along, going down Pacific and Nostrand Streets, I doubled stepped to keep up with him. He walked blindly and silently in anger to an unknown destination, occasionally bumping into the people he encountered without any consideration through the streets of Brooklyn.

Soon the moon shone its face and the two of us stood tired, hungry, alone, and confused. We stood in the subway station at the place of the L train, and there the station had become our home. It was twelve midnight and we looked so alone. It seemed that we did not even belong to each other. We waited in silence.

In a moment we heard footsteps, turned and caught the sight of an old, short, slow-moving figure, it approached us. As the figure moved toward us, wearing dark pants and shirt and a hat pulled over the dark skin, we could see it was the figure of a woman. The balls of her eyes appeared even darker against the contrast of the white eyes shining from under the rim of the hat she wore.

It seemed she came out of nowhere – and there she stood near us – detached. But she soon spoke, breaking the silence.

"What are you kids standing out here this time of night for?" She questioned.

Somehow the woman sensed the trouble of the two. Her natural instincts had figured it all out. Our being here revealed something was not right—not with the two alone, so young and here in the middle of the night with a child.

"Where are you going?" She questioned again.

The two of us stared at the lady without words. For a quick and hot moment, my body tingled with the instant impulse to burst into tears and run into the lady's arms for consoling—to tell her all that had happened. I made a desperate effort to control my emotions. I fought back the tears and sadness I felt.

Walter spoke. He, at first stuttered when he did speak. "We, we, were just standing here, ah, trying to think of what we wanted to do." His voice became more controlled now. He seemed to be the Walter that I wanted him always to be—gentle, kind and warm. And he knew how to be that way when he wanted to be.

"Where do you live?" She asked, as she stood there eyeing the three of us.

"We, ah, don't have a place. I mean we just came here from North Carolina, and we had a little "thang" while ago with the woman we were living with, so we had to leave, and we really don't have a place. You Know what I mean? P-u-u-u-u-u-u." Walter sighed, giving the lady a little sad smile. He placed his arm around Raven and me.

"I'm not worried 'bout myself," he started, placing his hand in his pocket and teetering from his heals to his toes two or three times. Lifting his head, he continued, "I could sleep anywhere, but you see we got this little baby here." He drew a deep breath and released it.

The lady leaned over to look at Raven. I pulled the pink colored blanket which wrapped the baby to expose her tiny head. Raven was wide-eyed and peering back at the lady.

"Oh look at you," she said touching the baby's head. "Keep her covered up it's chilly tonight."

I arranged the blanket around Raven

The lady began again, "I'm Clara Willis, and I'm on my way home from work. Why don't you stay at my place tonight?" Clara spoke with a sharp Brooklyn accent. Her voice was sincere.

Walter readied for his opportunity like a puppy about to grab a biscuit. He took her up on her offer. "Do you think it will be all right? I mean, uh, where do you live?"

Clara explained, "I live on Nostrand and 37 Avenue. We'll have to take the "L" Train to Nostrand and transfer."

Walter, now showing some concern, some shyness, a contradiction to the way he was before, asked his question, "Will your husband mind?"

"I don't have a husband, Honey." She spoke without any signs of pain or despair in her voice, and she seemed the kind of woman that could handle things when she said what she said. She ran her hand inside her pocket and pulled out some money. "Here, take this change and go and buy some tokens for yourselves."

Walter accepted the money, thanked her, and walked away to buy the tokens without another word. I stood silently. I thought that this lady might take us home with her, introduce us to some friends and ask us to stay for a while. I hoped that this lady would be kind and sensitive and say, why don't you stay here a while until you get on your feet – find yourself a place to stay? And we would stay for a while. I could clean the house and cook the meals while Walter and Clara worked. The arrangement would be perfect for all. I thought.

"Is the baby all right?" Clara questioned with genuine concern in her voice.

"Yes, she's okay." I said.

"Would you like me to hold her for a while?" She asked.

I was delighted for Clara to take the baby. I was exhausted, hungry and sleepy, I felt on the verge of collapsing. We had walked such a long, long way, and all I thought of was crawling lazily between some clean sheets and falling silently asleep, until daylight, when I would awaken to a meal and bath. I handed Raven to the lady with relief and trust.

The two room apartment loomed in the basement of an old building, and it held a dark underground air with dark colors and a dusty odor. A huge bed monopolized its space. Glass trinkets of odd shapes and colors filled two wall shelves and lined a narrow window base. The space was clearly provided for the individual dwelling there.

Clara locked the door behind us and beckoned us to make ourselves comfortable. "The three of you can use the bed, and I'll sleep in the kitchen."

"Won't you be uncomfortable there? We don't mind sleeping on the floor. We are just happy to have a roof over our heads."

Inside my heart, I felt happy for having Walter say kind words to Clara showing some gratitude. Ironically, although we had just met her, and she lived in a sort of dungeon, I felt safe here. At least we were off the streets.

I felt safe because the dwellings were so much like what I had already known. They reminded me of home- the drabness of the living quarters—the crowded space, and yes, the absence of fresh air. I identified with it all. And this lonely person lived here. This nice lonely person—what had she done to deserve this? I sat on the bed and lay Raven beside me.

"Now, you go on and use the bed. Are you hungry? I can make you some eggs if you would like them."

I wanted desperately to eat—something! But I did not want to put Clara through any trouble.

"No thank you."

"It won't be any trouble now if you want to eat. I can rest tomorrow because I usually sleep late during the day. I don't have to be at work until six."

I agreed, "I'm not hungry," thinking that the hunger pains would disappear with sleep.

Clara exited to a small and dim hallway, and she could be heard laying her bed in the other part of the apartment—the kitchen. For a while there was silence and then, "Whew!" Nothing else was heard, and the lights went out.

****

When morning came Raven began to cry, and I arose to attend to her. Walter was awakened too by her cry and arose and dressed.

"I have to go to 39th Street to pick up a check from my old job. Emily, I want you to go with me." He turned to me now, "Do you think Mrs. Willis could keep Raven until we come back?"

"I don't know, maybe she will if we ask her." Inside I did not want to leave my baby, but I dared not disappoint Walter either. He knocked on the kitchen door, and Mrs. Willis appeared and stood there in her pajamas rubbing her red eyes.

"What's wrong?" She asked.

"Oh, nothing, I wanted to explain something to you and ask a favor."

"Okay, what is it?" She wanted to know.

When it was Walter's turn, he explained, "I have to go and pick up my check at 39th Street, and I wanted you to keep the baby for us until we come back. I'll pay you and we'll come right back as soon as I pick up my check and get it cashed."

"I guess it will be all right," she said willingly and rubbing her eyes again. "You sure you coming right back?"

"Oh yeah," Walter said looking her straight in the eyes.

"Well, okay. Do you have food for the baby and everything?" Mrs. Willis wanted to know as she watched me feed Raven.

"Oh sure, the baby's food is down here in a bag. But I'm sure we'll be back before she wants to eat again."

"Come on Emily; let's hurry so we can get back."
We thanked Mrs. Willis, and kissed Raven and we were
off.

****

The sun had disappeared, and I imagined Mrs.
Willis sat there staring at Raven crawling around on the
bed, asking herself, "Where in the world did your
parents go? I believe they have left you here for me to
keep. But, I can't keep a baby. I'll just have to call the
police, and tell them what happened," then picking up
the receiver, saying "Hello operator, this is an
emergency. I want to report an abandoned baby."

****

"Emily, we have to hurry; I'm sure Mrs. Willis
has wondered why we're not back yet." The subway
train had taken much longer than Walter anticipated.
We finally rushed to the door of Mrs. Willis' apartment.
Walter knocked on the door.

Immediately the door was opened and Mrs. Willis
stood there amazed, "Come on in." She closed the door,
"Oh God, I thought you weren't going to return. I was
afraid that you had left your baby!" She rubbed her
head with both hands.

I thought, what I imagined had actually
happened.

"What do you mean?" Walter began angrily.
"Where is Raven?" He stood with his hands on his hips
veering down at Mrs. Willis.

"She is with the police. I waited and waited for you two to return, and when you didn't, I called the police."

"The police? The POLICE!" Walter questioned like he was in total disbelief.

"I'm sorry, but like I told you," she said, turning to the window. I didn't know if you would come back for the baby." She tried to tell us.

Walter and I stood there bewildered and terrorized. "Where is the baby? I mean at what police station?"

Mrs. Willis turned around and handed Walter a paper, "Here is the address." She was almost in tears, and her hand shook when she handed him the address.

****

"Come on Emily." We dragged our tired bodies up to the desk where a husky, tall police sergeant stood at the police precinct.

He immediately looked up, "What can I do for you kids? He asked.

"Sir," Walter hesitated for a second, "I'm Walter Phifer and this is my wife Emily. We were told that our baby is here at this station." I stood there beside him in silence.

"Oh, yes, just a minute." He walked over to a desk and sat down.

Walter became impatient, "Is our baby here or not?" He questioned.

The officer looked up again and shuffled some papers on the desk, replied, "Yes, one of our men picked her up. You two were charged with abandoning your child." He looked from Walter to me and back to Walter again.

Before he could continue, Walter interrupted, "We didn't abandon our baby. I went to my job to pick up my check, and the woman was supposed to keep the baby until we returned. But instead, she called the police." He blurted out angrily, and breathing heavily.

"Well, calm down. You'll have to wait 'till morning. Nothing can be done tonight. In the morning, Mr. Jeffers will talk to you about it."

"Where is the baby?" Walter demanded an answer.

"Your baby is safe in a foundling hospital, and Mr. Jeffers will explain everything to you tomorrow. I suggest that you not worry about her. You should go home and come back in the morning." The officer explained as he stacked papers on his desk.

"We don't have a home—a place to go" Walter revealed to the officer, and then looked down at me. The look on his face was not the threatening one I saw when he was angry with Mrs. Randal—no, this was more like hurt and disappointment—almost fear. I associated this look with what I had seen the night I discovered him standing in the rain at our house in Morristown, on the day I first met him when he told me *if Larry won't marry you, then I will.*

The officer veered up once more and replied, "I suppose the two of you can wait over there on that bench until morning."

"Okay," the two of us turned and walked over to the bench in a daze.

The police station was cold, and by now it was very late. The one sergeant at the desk sat silently and mechanically about his work as Walter and I waited until morning for news about Raven.

The bench was narrow, and Walter laid my head on his lap with hope that I would rest. The minutes seemed like hours—hours seemed like days. The hardness of the bench pierced the very flesh and protruded right into the bones of our bodies. I was so, so tired, but sleep would not enter my soul. I tossed and turned to the torturous thoughts that twisted the thinking of my mind's eye of the events of the day. I was afraid of never seeing my baby again.

I thought how can I live without her; or what's more live with myself and Walter? I knew I should have never, NEVER left my baby. But what could I have done. Walter wanted to take me with him. I wanted sleep so badly. That way, I wouldn't have to think. I would not have to remember. I wouldn't have the pain. The images of Raven shot through my mind like lightening, and I became more restless—it was impossible.

My baby, my baby – my sweet little baby, I longed to hold her close to my breast, the way mothers hold their children, and make them know they are safe, secure and loved. The thoughts made me feel weak and helpless. I turned over and cuddled my face next to Walter's stomach as if he could make everything all right again. I finally drifted off to sleep.

****

"Walter Phifer and Emily Phifer," a voice called when I turned over and discovered a tall stout man wearing a grey suit and tie. He held a stack of papers in his hand. He was standing before us at the bench. "Are you Walter Phifer?" He asked.

"Emily, sit up now. Yes, I'm Walter Phifer – this is Emily." We both stood.

This man looked at us as if to look straight through us. His voice was strong, cold and insensitive—matter-of-factly when he spoke. "We have a charge against you for abandoning your baby. Come with me." He commanded. He led us down a long hallway to a small room with a desk and chair. He walked behind the desk and sat down. He told us, "Sit down." Then he asked, "You want to tell me what happened?"

"What happened?" Walter stood up, hesitated there for a while. Placing his hands in his pockets, he started in a monotonous voice, "We only asked *that* woman to keep our baby until we went to pick up my paycheck from my job. And when we got back, she told us our baby was here." He continued to talk underneath his breath—"That bitch!"

"What did you say? The man asked in surprise.

"Oh nothing," there was silence, and then, "Can we have our baby?"

"Please sit down." The man gestured to a chair with his hand. "Where do you live?" He asked and waited for an answer.

"Well, we don't have a - we're going to stay with these friends that live in the building where my sister lives."

"What are these people's names? He wanted to know.

"Ah, Mr. and Mrs. John Bradley." Walter claimed.

"You see Walter, we must confirm residency. You know you must have living quarters before we can return your baby to you. And if you don't have a place to stay, we will have to keep the baby in the hospital until you do." He explained as he shuffled his papers, and tilted his glasses. "If I could call the Bradley's and confirms what you have said…"

Walter scratched his head, "Well, you see actually, I was planning on asking them if we could stay there for a while, you know, until we find a place."

****

Two hours now had passed, and we sat bewildered, on a bench at the precinct. We sat homeless; our baby Raven now taken away and placed in a foundling hospital. We were the castaways, we were immoral, we were the babes of society's game— the game of survival of the fittest.

We sat there with our confused minds. What would we do? Where would we go? I thought back to Morristown—to my Mon and Dad's—I thought NEVER!

The precinct was musty and drab. This place seemed totally foreign to us and to what I had ever known. I had never been in a police station for any reason in my life. I longed eagerly for some human individual to appear, approach us and speak softly and kindly and say, what are you kids doing here? Why don't you come home with me?

"You two need to go home!" A voice said.

The two of us were bothered—startled when we peered up into the eyes of Walter's half sister, Lucille. She stood towering over us in a red dress. Her voice was icy and direct. She made her unconcerned statement, turned and disappeared through the door.

Walter had not seen his sister since being in New York, or for that matter for many years. Her appearance assured him that the family back home was now aware of the unfortunate predicament.   The terrible thought now was forced to the surface.

Walter sat there continuously rubbing his head. He seemed to now face the fear of returning home from the "big city" a failure. The thoughts raced through his mind at a speed which was uncontrollable to him. That would mean Emily would have to return to the eyes of the people she left and to the town of her *love.* If I let her go back for a month, until I get a job and a place, she could return to me. He thought. But *he* might be there while she was home. They might see each other. ***He*** might take her away from me. He jumped up from the bench and walked around in a circle.

I imagined he was telling himself, No! This was out of the question. The two of us must stick it out together. After all, we are married—man and wife. She is supposed to stay with me—her husband—she's carrying *my* baby now. He looked over at me. He seemed to say, he will not get his opportunity to achieve his vendetta against me. Walter's concern was primarily with triumph. In an abstract way, he loved me. But mostly, he adored the idea – the idea of taking me away from Larry, of having Larry's girl. He sat down on the bench beside me again wondering, with dark, wide eyes, looking across the room—daydreaming.

It seemed he had exchanged one mental hell for another—his exodus from home away from Larry to here.

Part VI
Walter's Other Side

*W*hen the news spread in the building in Brooklyn where Lucille lived, the Bradley's heard and came to our rescue. We were able to bathe our tired bodies and were fed at the kind people's apartment.

We were given a place to sleep on a single cot in the basement of the apartment building in the boiler room for a week, until Walter could find another job. He had already drawn his final pay check from his job at the hospital as an orderly. So he would need to find work right away.

In the boiler room the apartment dwellers stored their old clothing and unused furniture. It was dark and dusty and the fumes from the gigantic boiler which fired every four hours to heat the building with a thunderous roar filled the closed-in-dark hole in the ground.

This hole was not without other inhabitants of which Walter soon sought out and introduced to me. There was the couple who lived in the only basement complete apartment, who ate mostly Italian foods which the woman brought to me each night. And each night that she brought the food, I emptied it into a box in the closet and ate nothing all day for fear the food would make me ill. I had a strange feeling that I was disliked by this strange woman who I would hear often arguing with her husband about having affairs with other women, and who told the landlord, I later learned, that Walter had made a "pass" at her—which I learned, was an untruth and happened to be nothing more, according to Walter, than a compliment made to her about her cooking, one day while the three stood in the doorway for a brief chat. Retrospectively, I suppose she told her husband in an attempt to make him jealous so he would give her more attention.

The other inhabitant was an "invisible man" character who dwelled in a one room well lighted space. The room had shelves lined with record albums and pictures of famous sports figures such as Jackie Robinson, Joe Lewis and the like. My eyes flickered around at the objects which cluttered the room. And as I stared, the eyes from a portrait in a square frame of an old man seemingly sad stared back at me. The eyes in the portrait awakened some feeling of strange memories of home. Feeling them look back at me as if to reveal something naked about my existence in the room. The eyes seemed to say, I know you like the eyes in a portrait at my grandmother's house. The eyes in the portrait in the dining room they seem to follow my eyes—to warn me of some danger. But I refused to give in to the urge and want for home. I resisted the pain as though I was ashamed to acknowledge what I dared not think about—my mother's arms, my father's love—but I just couldn't handle the poverty—I just could not do it!

Forcing my eyes away, they fell upon several empty bottles which at one time had contained wine, some books about famous black men, and right above one fat anthology of Black Writers was a picture of Christ hung on the cross. I became dazed for a moment and overwhelmed with a feeling of homesickness. I swallowed and took a seat at the end of a huge bed.

I had never seen such a collection of things— records, pictures, books. This man worked at night and slept during the day. His space seemed to make other realities unreal like time standing still – as if there were no other world outside this one. He offered us a cigarette which he, himself, rolled.

This man and Walter smoked and the three of us were taken under the spell of either the cigarette or the melodic Blues—Nina Simone's "Mississippi Goddamn" which played softly in the background on the old phonograph. No one talked but entered a dreamlike reality – and I followed like Coleridge in *Kublai Khan.* I entered the woods of the pine trees, the horses, and the adventure of my younger years when my family lived on the old Charlotte Highway in the deep country.

--Oh Cisco…

--Oh Poncho…

I saw my Mexican lover ride through the woods. He swept me up on his horse and rode away into the deep woods. My hair parted down the middle, and two braids hung at my shoulders. I wore the soft moccasins over my small feet.

"I love you Senorita."

"I love you my Cisco."

My mind floated to my baby now. Now the image of Raven's face was clear.

"Mommy! Mommy!"

I imagined my baby holding out her small arms and crying. My mind floated to home where I felt my mother's hands picking me up into her arms and wiping away the tears.

"Don't cry baby."

"But Mama…"

"It will be all right."

"What's the matter wid' her?"

"She's just crying."

"What for? Did somebody do something to her?"

"No, she's all right. Go back to sleep!"

"Emily, Emily! Come on in now, it's dark out there girl. Emily, where are you?"

"Thomas, now don't get mad, but Emily's gone have a baby."

"What? I knew that boy's been hanging around here too much. Well, what's she gonna do?"

I suddenly thought back to the time of my school days and Mrs. Carlson who used to loosen my braids and comb them--and how my oldest sister Ruth was referred to as my sister instead of my being referred to as Ruth's sister because I was the "light-skinned" one with the long hair.

--Oh Cisco…

--Oh Poncho…

Mama used to say, "Do you think you're light skinned. And I would feel confused and uneasy about my mother's comment. I felt an unjustifiable flaw in the work of Mother Nature in our differences. I felt discrimination from my own mama and sister – I felt the outsider.

"You're not that much lighter than your sister… Let me see your arm."

I thought of my house cleaning and ironing job at Mrs. Honeysuckle's. The way her house smelled of fruit, roses and the way the wash smelled when it's stayed on the line during a spring rain. The hard wood shinny floors that you see your face in if you get close enough.

"What are you doing out of school, Emily...?"

"I'm going to have a baby..."

"Why you poor thing..."

"Are you married...?"

"No."

I thought of how Ruth and I had walked to the white folk's house and how I had worked all day – scrubbing, cleaning and ironing all those starched shirts when the good white lady had said: "Here's four dollars, Honey."

When the white woman offered me the four dollars, I felt cheated of the opportunity to reveal how much I would charge. I felt harmed. I expected much more.

"Four dollars? I expected much more, at least ten."

"Ten dollars?" She asked as if out of the question.

"Uh huh." I replied—"Ten."

Mr. Homesuckle sat there amazed at the fact that a little poor Black girl could think or even possessed a mind. And what's worse, that she could think of disagreeing. She could think of some profit?

He immediately jumped to "Miss Ann's" defense, as if to say—the very idea of expressing a difference of opinion toward this "pure" lady was unheard of. "I'll take you home Ruth. And Emily you can walk."

That's one thing about the Southern white man during the white Supremacy era; he wanted to, by any means necessary, keep those "ni-----" in their place. He defended his kind, right or wrong.

Ruth just stood there amazed at my attitude and nerve. Declining the ride, she and I walked home together in complete silence.

I took Ruth's silence as an example of her loyalty to the white folks and that she sided with them. When we arrived home, I was feeling tired; I had gone straight to bed. Ruth had not wasted any time telling Mama on me. Mama stormed into the bedroom furiously.

"What do you mean going around telling people you gone have a baby? Don't you know it is a disgrace for an unmarried girl to have a baby?"

I was afraid, confused tired and sleepy. I remained silent. All I was, was a little fifteen year old baby myself, about to have a baby and not knowing how to respond when people asked me about it. Was I supposed to lie? I just didn't know anything. And nobody was concerned enough to tell me. Evidently I assumed Mama felt that Mrs. Homesuckle had talked to Ruth about my revealing the pregnancy, and she had been ashamed of me.

My mind floated on to the Standridges and that big pink baby I used to take care of that was so huge I could hardly pick him up from his crib, being the small frail girl that I was. My memory stirred up the indignation I had felt toward Mrs. Standridge the time I overheard a conversation between the white lady that I worked for and the lady's husband.

I had gone home and repeated it to Walter. The neighbor had said that Mr. Standridge was ill of his own doings, seeing that he was an alcoholic, and one who kept the car out half the night.

God punished him for his wrongdoings, it seemed. The next day, Mrs. Standridge saw fit to pick me up in the big car – to explain about her husband, and how the things I heard couldn't have possibly been about Mr. Standridge.

Mrs. Standridge had tried to explain how her husband was a good man, and that people wanted to hurt them. The big car had glided along the road as Mrs. Standridge talked. I remembered my smallness as I sat there listening. I remembered the fear I felt and the anxiety of wanting to reveal what I felt was the truthfulness of the conversation I overheard, especially since I had myself seen the Standridge car parked at the house of Saphronia, who lived right down the street from Grandma AJ, about dawn on several mornings. I remembered Grandma AJ and Mae Raleigh talking about it.

I dared not contradict the powerful woman for fear of getting myself and Walter fired. Oh yes, I felt indignation toward Walter's disloyalty too. Yes, Walter! I thought of lying on the little bed in the same room where I had to sleep in the room with Mama and Daddy when Raven was born, and my being afraid to send for Walter the morning of the birth for fear he would not come.

He had struck me several times in the face when we argued. Walter had said that my mama didn't want me. I called him a liar, and he struck me hard and then took his clothes and left me to go back to his parents'.

Ruth told him about the baby being born, and eventually he did come and the three of us moved in with his family.

I thought of how impressed I had been with Mrs. Phifer being a school teacher. The impression of this woman had opened my eyes to ideas and possibilities which had never occurred to me before. For example, what I wanted to make of myself. I decided, and it would be so. I would be a teacher like his mother. I would teach and take care of my little baby, Raven. I did not know how I would do it, but it would be so.

I thought of how at first Walter and I lived a playhouse fantasy—two children playing house. But soon I discovered that Walter had a serious drinking problem. We fought and constantly required the supervision of his mother. His temper flared up and he communicated with his fist on the slightest contradiction to his way.

Mr. Phifer was a working man, but he hardly ever spent much of his time at home. He often came home late at night and argued at his wife for no apparent reason. When he did this, he was usually intoxicated. Mr. Phifer had a power struggle with his wife because she was professional and he was blue collar. He worked for the influential Whites in town including the Mayor, and this he tried to use to establish his dominance and importance at home. He could be heard telling his wife, "You think you know everything—you don't know *nothing*!"

After Walter dropped out of Johnson C. Smith University in his sophomore year and after marrying me he did so without his parents' knowledge. They were the kind of parents, I believe, would have tried and never given their consent to marry me—not carrying another man's child. When his mother first discovered his possible marriage, she went looking for him at one of his best friend's Jake McMillan's house. When Walter heard his mother's voice, he and I having been there at the time, we hid in Jake's bedroom and Jake's sister Mattie lied for us saying we were not there. Mrs. Phifer asked if Walter was married, that she had heard he was. And after Mae Raleigh and Grandma AJ confirmed the news to the community, their family did come to see me.

Walter felt himself to be better than I, partly because his mother was a teacher and partly because he lived in a large home, graduated from high school and attended college.

Once again, the indignation swelled in my chest when I thought of how Walter had forced my head down to kiss the kitchen floor of his parents' home. He said he had done me a favor by marrying me, and that I had better worship the house and thank my lucky stars. After all, my mother had put her own daughter out of the house.

He said this because Mama locked the screen door once when I stayed out past eleven o'clock with Walter. That night Walter had taken me to a dark room and taken advantage of me—it could have been charged as rape—him being nineteen and I fifteen. I didn't tell him no. How could I? No one had ever instructed me to say no!

At that moment, I *despised* Walter. But what could I do? I did not want to return to the poverty which I experienced at my parents' house.

I did return to my parents' just once when I was very young, perhaps before age eighteen when I made an attempt to leave Walter while we lived in Morristown. I had taken a job downtown at Quick's Canteen as a waitress, cooking hamburgers, preparing dinner plates, and washing dishes for one dollar an hour. Walter made it impossible to work. He would just show up at my job and stand around at the door directing expression of "hate" on his face toward me and talk to himself. One of the black cooks, the one called Big Six and the other one I cannot recall, anyway, she told me one morning, "You know he's going to hurt you." So out of fear for my life, I returned to Mrs. Phifer's

This one time that I did return I discovered the bed bugs (chinches), had had a call meeting and decided that there was some fresh blood in the house. They set up a picnic on my body. One morning when I arose, to say the least, I was alarmed by and ashamed of the itchy red dots from insect bites on my arm across my back that led to my other arm. I couldn't stand it. So, I made up my mind then that I would never, ever return, especially once I left and became exposed to the simple amenity of a bathtub with real running hot water, that was it, and I really meant it. I don't know which one was worse, Walter or the chinches. **Anything was better than the bedbugs. Therefore, I chose the deep blue sea.**

My thoughts now wandered back to Larry and my love for him. That as sure as spring turns into winter, that our love would wither and die. Why had he gone away and left me when I love and needed him so much. The pain cut like a sharp blade through my memory and in my heart. I made a sigh and was brought back from my dreams to reality—the here and now when Walter said, "Come on Emily, I'll take you to the room so you can get some sleep." He walked me to our hole in the ground.

Part VII
Lucille's News

*W*hen I awoke the next morning, with thoughts of the night before still in my head, Walter was nowhere in sight. The night before Walter had brought me to the cot, but he must have gone out again, perhaps returned to the man's room. But why? I got up out of bed and dressed. The door opened and it was Walter. He was smiling.

"I've been upstairs to Jan's." his other half sister who also lived in the building. "She said that we can come up to eat breakfast and take a bath. Come on." He said with a slight jerk of his head.

Thoughts rushed through my head back to the time at the precinct when Lucille, Jan's sister, had appeared and warned us to return home. I wondered if Jan was anything like her sister Lucille. I thought, she couldn't be because she was trying to do something good. She was being kind. So I dressed and prepared to go up and meet Jan at her apartment.

Jan was a school teacher in the New Your City school district for many years. She was twenty-one years older than Walter and she and her sister Lucille were the children from his father's first marriage. Both Lucille and Jan were single women with no children.

Jan's apartment was spacious and brightly decorated with plush upholstered chairs, heavy colorful drapery with cornices that covered huge windows overlooking the city, and ceramics and crystal lined a marble fireplace and shelves held thick books; paintings hung on almost every wall.

The aroma of bacon and eggs filled the air and made me feel so good. As Walter and I entered the kitchen Jan said, "Come on in here to the table."

There sat Lucille sitting at the table. She eyed us like a wolf about to pounce upon its prey. Her stare seemingly penetrated the very skin as she looked the kind of well-look-who-we-have-here look. Walter eyed her back steadily, and she did not speak as we took a seat at Jan's table. I felt an instant sickness beginning to grow inside—perhaps from morning sickness or from the sight of Lucille. I did not want to face her.

Jan stood in front of the kitchen stove scrambling some eggs. She turned and grinned at the two of us, "I'm glad you came. I hope you're hungry?"

Lucille's stare intensified, and she readied for her attack. "You didn't know what you were getting into with this boy, did you?" She continued maliciously before either of us could respond. "Did he tell you about how he worried his mother *all* the time—always getting into trouble—stealing purses, throwing rocks at cars...?"

Tears filled my eyes.

Lucille continued, "He didn't finish college because he was too busy socializing at the clubs and spending his mother's hard-earned money. He isn't worth a dime. I don't know what you wanted to marry him for."

I couldn't take it anymore. I started. "They kept our baby because we didn't have a place to stay. You could have helped you know."

Lucille was shocked by these words. She sprang up from the table and went over to the stove and spit into the pan of eggs which Jan was preparing. She made a twirl away from her vicious destruction, and I caught sight of the red underwear and the gigantic dark brown heave Amazon thighs underneath her wide-tail-devil-blue dress as she threw her weight from left to right like an animal out of control. She fled from the kitchen and out of the apartment.

Walter turned immediately, shoved his hands into his pockets and walked away from the kitchen. He left the apartment and me sitting there.

Jan took the pan of eggs over to the garbage can and emptied them there. "Don't worry, I have plenty of eggs. I'll just make some more. Lucille shouldn't have done that. She went over to the refrigerator, gathered more eggs and prepared to break them in a bowl.

I sat amazed at Lucille, not knowing what to do or say. I didn't feel much like eating now—not after this. I pulled myself together to be able to speak. "I'm not hungry now. I want to go back downstairs."

"Don't let Lucille get you upset. She gets like that every now and then. You need to eat some food before you make yourself sick. Stay here now and eat." She went on making breakfast as if nothing had happened.

A sound was heard by the two of us who sat picking over our plates of bacon, eggs, toast and orange slices. It was Walter returning. I could finally eat, finally!

****

Two weeks later, Walter was now working again second shift from three until eleven pm at the local hospital; living in the basement made it possible for us to get Raven back from the foundling hospital. I would spend my days in the little room with my baby, and go out for one meal a day when Walter returned home from work.

Raven was now nine months old and able to stand—say Mama. I knew the little knot in the bottom of my stomach which had previously revealed my pregnancy with Raven was growing rapidly. It had been three months since I had seen my period.

****

It was now 3:00 a.m. and Walter was not home yet. I tried desperately to sleep to fight away the pains of hunger. If he were to get out of a car or stumble down the steps, he could not be heard over the roar of the broiler.

At 4:00 a.m. Walter's keys were finally heard in the door as he dragged himself in and turned on the light. He smelled heavily of alcohol. He mumbled something to himself, as he flop his intoxicated body down on the cot and pulled his shoes off.

I was afraid to see him this way. "Where have you been? I was worried about you." I spoke in a timid voice—asking a question any wife would have a natural right to ask of her husband coming home at this hour when he is usually home at 11:30 p.m.

He turned to look at me. "What the hell do you mean, where have I been? He snickered, "I've been out! Where have you been?" He asked in a cynical tone. He proceeded to undress and half way through he mumbled, "That mother-fuckin bastard! I hope I broke his jaw!"

With his pants pulled down around his ankles, he fell across the foot of the cot into an intoxicated sleep. It was Walter's regular pay day, and I was tempted to look through his pockets to see if he had his money. I abandoned the idea for fear he would awaken and catch me.

Even if I found the money, where would I go at this hour to eat? Someone might harm me in the streets alone. I couldn't take my baby out either, and something might happen to her if I leave her here alone with Walter sleeping like this. There was nothing I could do except wait until daylight.

I curled my body into a fetal position for want of my mother's arms and some warm grits with butter. Snarl...snarl the cramps in my stomach seemed to ease in this position. I drifted off thinking of home and what Walter had said.

One eye and three eyes had beautiful clothes and they ate the best of food. But little two eye had to eat the scraps from the table. She was made to do all of the chores while her sisters played outside in the sun.

Rope, rope, hang the butcher so butcher will kill ox and ox will drink water and water will put out fire...

Mama tell us the story about the rich lady and the poor old lady...

Once upon a time there was a rich old lady and a very poor lady. They lived in the same town, and one day a beggar came knocking at the door of the old lady's house; and although she did not have an abundance of food, she shared what she had with the beggar. So, before the beggar left, he told the old lady, "Whatever you do the first thing tomorrow morning, you will continue to do it all day. The poor old lady did not remember what the man had said. But the very next morning when she arose, she began to count her pennies to buy some bread. A miracle happened, as she counted, her money began to multiply. She counted money all day and became rich. When the news spread to the rich old lady's house she found the beggar, invited him in and fed him the best of food—a meal fit for a king. So, before the beggar left, he said, "The first thing you do tomorrow morning, you will continue to do all day."

When the beggar left, the rich lady couldn't wait for morning so she stayed up all night making boxes and sacks for her money; therefore, she spent the entire day making boxes and sacks.

Now I was flying. I was the best—sweeping down low and up high over the tall buildings. I loved to fly. And right before falling out of the air—before hitting the ground...

There was a loud yell. Raven was awake and crying. I sprang up in bed with the fear of hitting the ground still in my mind. I crawled out of bed. The story of one eye, two eyes, and three eyes continually raced through my mind. I went over to the large stroller where Raven stood crying and picked her up.

Raven's crying woke Walter, and the noise seemed to anger him when he arose. His red eyes searched about the room in a disoriented sense of a foreign place. His bearings took grip when his eyes found the baby and me. He sat up on the bed still in a foul mood from the intoxication of the night before and loss of sleep. His voice cracked when he growled, "What time is it?"

"Seven forty-five? I answered.

"Can't you keep that baby quiet?" he cruelly asked.

"She's crying because she's hungry and wet. And I'm hungry too, Walter."

Taking hold of himself, he sat up straight on the bed and held his head in his hands. Finally he stood and pulled his pants up to hide his nakedness. His head seemed to spin, as he stumbled a little before flopping back down on the bed. Seemingly to remember the events of the night before, he examined his hand and then his pockets. He began, "I lost my job Emily... but it was not my fault. This mother-fucker called me a nigger, and I hit him. I hope I broke his mouth. I knew they were goin' to fire me, so I left before the boss got a chance to tell me I was fired."

I listened to Walter's story as I fed Raven from the baby food jar that I warmed in a pan of hot water sitting on an electric hot plate. I was bewildered. What would I do now? It might take weeks before Walter finds another job—perhaps months. The authorities might find out. And we certainly couldn't live in this unhealthy environment much longer with a baby. How would we live?

Walter reached into his pockets and brought out four ten dollar bills. He now looked at me, "Here is some money. I guess I spent the rest. We'll have to call Mama collect, and ask her to wire us some money. I can make the call from Jan's."

I finished feeding Raven and kissed her. "Okay baby girl, now you're all right." Placing her in the stroller, I walked over to the corner where the cardboard suitcase sat. I placed it on the bed and began to put my few belongings inside.

"What are you doing? What are you doin' Emily?" Walter's surprised tone frightened me, but I kept on packing.

"I'm leaving. I'm using this money to buy a bus ticket to my uncle's in New Jersey."

"New Jersey? What uncle? You mean you're leaving me?"

I started to pack Raven's clothes.

"I love you Emily. You can't leave. I won't let you." He began to rip my clothes off. "You're going back to Larry! That's where you're going!"

I screamed, "Stop it Walter!" I started to cry from fear, pain, hunger, exhaustion and want of protection. "Oh Jesus!" I cried and He must have heard me.

Walter grabbed me but different from before and held me tightly in his arms. "I'll go with you. I'll get another job, you'll see. I'll make it all up to you Pumpkin. You'll see." He started to try and put the pieces of my blouse back together like one would put the pieces of a puzzle together. He too, began to cry.

Mentally, I knew a trip from New York to New Jersey, and not actually knowing where to go—how to find Uncle Hector, my daddy's brother, could be a frightening experience for a fifteen year old teenager on the streets along with a baby. But I was determined to leave this hole in the ground. I hugged Walter back and felt his tears on my cheek. I could not hurt him this way. I released myself from his hold, stood and changed my blouse. I used the water in which I heated Raven's food, and wet a cloth to wash my face. Afterward, I turned to Walter, who sat on the cot with his head hung low.

"My mother sent Uncle Hector's address and telephone number. I'm going to call him from the telephone booth on the corner and let him know we're coming to Patterson."

111

Walter, was still pleading desperately, said, "Well, I'm going with you."

Part VIII
New Jersey

*W*e took the evening Greyhound to
Patterson, and from there the city bus to Maggie and my
uncle Hector's place.   Patterson was much like
Morristown – the small houses and streets with no
sidewalks. But there were many differences too—the
bars. There was a bar with glairing red and blue lights
directly across the street from the apartment house
where Maggie lived. The music could be heard clearly
up until early morning. The woman and men came and
went in their elaborate clothes as if they had nothing else
to do.

Maggie was a tall very dark skinned heavy-set
woman appearing to be well into her forties with four
children of her own, two girls who lived at home. Uncle
Hector was an average height, heavy built, very fair-
skinned, straight hair, green-eyes, ladies' man. He was
an Infrastructure worker on roads, highways and
bridges—what the locals called a "Hard Hat." It was
said of him that he carried pay checks from last year's
work around in his pocket. He was a "womanizer" and
like all his women jet black—seemed he felt there was
something to the old adage "the blacker the berry the
sweeter the juice."

He spoke swiftly with a sharp Northern accent—
dragging some of his syllables out at the end of his
phrases for emphasis—a part of his dialectic speaking

patterns and upbringing from the South. Uncle Hector speeded around the city in his red and white "Duce-and-a-quarter automobile"

After being at Maggie's in Patterson for three days, two of my cousins, Barbara and Rae from Morristown came up to Patterson to visit for the rest of the summer.

Maggie did domestic work during the day, and the young folk left there at the house during the day would play records, practice the latest dances, things that young people did in the 60s to have fun—the clean and innocent kind—not getting high on drugs or alcohol—or smoking cigarettes. I don't ever remember a single one of us indulging in any of those vices. Barbara, Ray, Maggie's two daughters, Mickey and Deloris their brother Robert and I spent lots of time dancing—cutting up and acting silly—making up steps to dances— sometimes we played card games: Bid Whist or Gin Rummy—Robert would occasionally bring one of his male friends with him. The latest dance at the time was the Hustle. Robert would say, "Let me show you how to do the Hustle," as he put Fat's Domino's "I'm Walking" on the record player. He began to demonstrate the dance. We all got into a line and he would be in front demonstrating.

Walter was as usual still in bed since he had been out late the night before at the bar across the street. When the music awakened him; he entered the room, viewed Robert and his friend with their arms around me and the others practicing the Hustle. He became irate; he immediately walked up to Robert pointed his finger in his face threatening him—"Don't you ever put your hands on my wife! Do you hear me? Don't you ever touch her!"

Everyone including me was shocked and I especially was ashamed.

"Walter, we were only dancing," Robert tried to tell him.

Walter veered at me, turned to point his finger at Robert again; he repeated, "Don't you ever put your hands-on-my-wife." He stalked out of the room with both fists clenched, and a few seconds later his voice was heard from the other room, "Emily, come in here!"

The house was quiet now with astonishment and disbelief except for the record which had stopped and needed the arm removed from it.

I went to Walter's command reluctantly—he called me into the room to have sex with me—sex that I did not want nor desire—therefore, I went through the motions, but I felt nothing—I felt absolutely powerless. As I think of it now, retrospectively, there is only an empty feeling of sadness that comes over my mind regarding that experience. The stench of his fluids only made me want to GAG! I was the mother of a child, and carrying another one in my womb, but I now know that I was still a virgin.

****

Fall had arrived and my trip to Patterson in my eyes had promised to be one of some protection. I soon realized my instincts to be wrong. My uncle offered no feelings of security. He was in and out of at least two girlfriend's houses, and the two were well known to the other. I took Raven and soon left Maggie's due to a quarrel Uncle Hector had with Walter about his hanging out at the bar.

Uncle Hector's other lady friend resembled Maggie extremely. She lived alone and allowed my

uncle to come and go as he pleased. She was kind and accepted Raven and me. One night when Walter had struck me, I took Raven and walked across the park to Uncle Hector's. Walter showed up the next day. He went out during the day in an endeavor to find work.
And eventually he did get a job with the Patterson Sanitation Department.

Through his job, Walter met some wonderful and generous people, the Brewers, who owned a home on Euclid Street still in Patterson but on the other side of town—the residential side with nice large homes, and sidewalk streets. They had a vacant room on the third floor with cooking facilities and bath. Walter rented it, and we shared the cooking facilities and bath with the other roomers on that floor. There was Pete and Margie, a married couple in one room, a young single man, Bobby, who worked at the downtown bakery, still in another room. After moving in, I kept to myself, and never said more than "Good morning", or "Hello" and "Thank you" to the occupants who lived in the house. I spent my days cooking and cleaning, watching the fetus develop and taking care of Raven, who was now walking. – I waited patiently for the day close to my delivery of the new baby, because I joyously knew I would return to Morristown, to Walter's parents' to have the baby.

Walter usually arrived home at four for a home cooked meal. But as time passed, he began arriving home hours later and later. I never gave it much thought, even though he was usually drinking when he arrived home.

And soon the swelling, and the itching, and the burning occurred. I could not imagine what it was that caused so much itching until it swelled and pained. I washed and rubbed in alcohol the best I could, but still it would not go away.   IGNORANCE IS A BLIND PIG--AN INVISIBLE DEMON THAT CAUSES DESRUCTION WITHOUT HAVING TO GIVE ANY REASON OR ANSWER TO ANY CONSEQUENSES OF JUSTICE. And a sixteen year old, coming from a poverty stricken Negro family who had not informed the babe about the **beast** in the woods of whom she should have been afraid, is easy prey, even to her own husband.

The itching was usually more persistent and painful at night when I slept in bed with Walter. And eventually I lay sprawled open with a mirror to view this part of my body. When I did, my heart skipped a beat and my mind raced with fear to see the swelling that had taken place from the scratching. "Oh God!"

Walter lay beside me in the two-by-four room in a deep alcoholic sleep. Raven lay at the foot of the bed in the corner near the wall. I prayed to God to let it go away. I dared not ask Walter about it—I was afraid. I did not want my eyes bruised and my nose injured. It was nothing for him to strike me for simply saying something he did not like, even though I was carrying a baby. And if I attempted to strike him back in defense, it only served to escalate the incident.

I knew for sure he possessed two personalities; I did not want to be the object of his alter ego's rages— his second self; the side that he tried to hide from other people until he couldn't keep it in.

Miraculously, the itching and swelling subsided. By now I was big with the baby I was carrying. So I prepared by washing up all the dirty clothes in a bathtub on my knees scrubbing them on a washboard and hung them on a clothesline that extended out of the window of the bathroom. And soon the day did arrive when Raven and I did return to Morristown for the delivery of the new baby.

It wasn't long, just two weeks later when Walter quit his job at the Patterson Sanitation Department and soon followed me to home in Morristown, during the middle of the cold month of January.

****

At age sixteen, I gave birth to a healthy baby girl we named Priscilla. And within four months, I found my belly growing big with another child.

I went to my mother and Mrs. Phifer hoping for some advice on how to keep from getting pregnant again. Mrs. Phifer told me she had five. And after all we don't have any boys. My mother told me she used a diaphragm. Well, I knew that didn't work because she had eleven children, and numerous miscarriages.

Walter had now decided he could provide better for his family by going to Washington, DC to find work.

He soon found work at Fort Myers in Arlington, Virginia. Walter soon sent a friend of his who lived in Washington, who had relatives in Morristown, and who also knew his family, the Phifers well; following their visit, on the way back to Washington, these friends picked up Raven, age one year and a half; and Priscilla, who was now nine months, and me; we rode back to Washington with them.

Walter shared a basement apartment with the janitor named David in an apartment building on New Hampshire Avenue in Northwest, Washington. The tenants who lived upstairs were white well-to-dos, and I soon became acquainted with the Rigby's. One afternoon Mrs. Rigby called David in search of someone who could help her with some house cleaning. I answered the call, talked to Mrs. Rigby and told her "I'm expensive."

Old man Rigby got a big chuckle out of that. He had been listening on the other end of the telephone. Mrs. Rigby worked for Continental Airlines, and Mr. Rigby was confined to a wheelchair. During the day while Mrs. Rigby was at work, his time was spent playing companion to his two white doves he allowed to fly freely about the apartment. When I did any kind of work for them, Walter came with me. Mr. Rigby delighted in teasing me because I was young—he often made little sexual innuendoes regarding, I supposed, what he missed now that he was restricted to a wheelchair—innuendoes I never paid any attention— and surprisingly neither did Walter. I supposed Walter knew he was no threat. His wife, Mrs. Rigby would often tell him, "I've just gotten off from work, and I am entitled to a little peace and quiet—I suppose she meant from the birds and from his constant attempt at humor. He did not try to hide the fact that he enjoyed his alcohol and his sense of humor. "His reply to her would be, "You're entitled to the whole god-dang bedroom. So get in there and be quiet." Through the Rigby's I became acquainted with the neighbor across the hall from them, Mrs. Trusedale, a single woman--a Catholic nurse.

Two months after I arrived in Washington with the children, Walter lost his job at Fort Myers; and we had to move from New Hampshire Avenue. He attempted to get his job back by insisting that I go to his former boss at Fort Myers and plead his case. I believe

Walter felt that the sight of a pregnant mother would gloss over his actions, and change the impression he left behind. We took a taxicab to the company. Walter waited outside while I went into Mr. Ahsur's office where he had been a male secretary's assistant. The Asian gentleman in his apology explained that once a decision was made, they were not in the habit of rescinding it. He said, "I'm so very sorry Mrs. Phifer, but Walter's insubordination and threat were grounds for legal actions against him. He lost his temper and threatened a supervisor here. So he was asked to leave and not return. I sincerely hope he will be able to secure other employment. But there is nothing that can be done. Good bye and good luck to you and Mr. Phifer." So my plea for Walter to have a second chance was to no avail.

****

Walter managed to secure employment at one of the local restaurants as a cook and waiter. He found us dwellings in one room of a house on Sixteenth Street with shared cooking facilities in the kitchen, still in Northwest Washington. A young girl and her husband had a room in the building. She kept Raven and Pricilla while I was hospitalized. I soon gave birth to our third child, Dawn, at Georgetown University Hospital.

When I was released, on the third day from the hospital, I could not bring Dawn home with me because of her breeched delivery—her feet came out of the womb first. The doctor kept putting his fingers up into my rectum several time, trying to turn her around so she would have a normal delivery, but he couldn't manage to turn her before she was born. So she had to remain in an incubator in the hospital for four days until her feet were their normal color. When we brought her home, Dawn was fine, and healthy with a beautiful head of curly hair.

The Rigby's neighbor, Mrs. Trusedale had a sister who was a nun who provided baby clothes, bottles, a crib—everything the baby could possible need. And after I brought Dawn home, they all came to our one room on Sixteenth Street to visit—the Rigby's, Mrs. Trusdale, David, and Mrs. Trusedale's sister the nun. They talked of how beautiful the baby and I were, how perfect my teeth were, how pretty my hair was—they could not pay us enough compliments. I felt very fortunate to have met such benevolent people who thought nothing of the color of my light brown skin— they saw me as a human being—a young woman in need.

By the time Dawn was three months, Walter lost his cooking job at the restaurant. I called his mother, Mrs. Phifer in Morristown, explained the situation— asked her to send money for a ticket so the children and I could return home—she did not hesitate—she wired the money for a bus ticket home.

While Walter lay sleeping off intoxication from the night before, I often lay in bed wishing I could go home—home to Mama and Daddy, to a warm, clean bed, love and protection. But I knew that did not exist. I would think of how Mama pedaled that old Singer sewing machine making our clothes, worked outside the home when she was not pregnant with another baby. *I did not wish to be like her*. My father, on the other hand was an educated, brilliant man, but *I just could not be like him either*, he tried to use his educational skills to better himself and his family. He was a World War II veteran; after he came home from the Army in 1942, he spent his entire life laboring on upholstery, because it was necessary for him to work three jobs to halfway feed all of his children. Sometimes after work, after his second job, when he wasn't working in his two-by-four upholstery shop he built in the back yard, with the little time he did have during the week, he created a blue print of a dream home that he was never able to build for his family. I can only imagine how that must have felt in the heart of such a bright man. On the weekend, we children on many occasions had to endure the ordeals of our parents' unpredictable and pathetic behavior.

At the end of a long work week **On many Saturday nights in our house, all Mom and Dad had was a pint of Seagram's Seven, a forty-five record, the occasional luxury of a can of oyster stew and each other**. Fatigue for Dad set into his soul after working three jobs during the week and I believe despair cut into his heart from "not having" that led to alcohol abuse. It was such an oxymoronic experience, although it brought about fights with Mom when they were not in bed making love, Daddy still found time on many Sunday mornings to flip pancakes and take them in to Mom. So—in between Daddy's responsibility to provide for his children and his endeavor to be a husband to Mama, there wasn't much time for raising us, or seeing that we were washed and cared for; knew our ABCs, so to speak. What we learned from them was absorbed by being around them. We mostly raised ourselves! At times, out of frustration, my dad's way of disciplining his children was calling us "A bunch of sap-headed idiots," and a "pack of heathens." Mama was overwhelmed from so many childbirths and miscarriages, and trying to work in between, she often suffered with postpartum depression which led her to sometimes mistreat us too. Her way of chastising us was, as she put it, "beat" the living shit out of us, "slap" the shit out of us for mostly anytime she felt we needed to be punished. In other words, we knew not to try that again or we knew what we would get from Iron-hand Mom.

Life in the fifties for Black folks was hard and without a professional career money was scarce. My parents met, and Mama fell in love head over hills in junior high school. They married shortly after graduation. Daddy had to marry Mama. She literally bullied and chased away any females that showed an iota of an interest in the straight-haired light-skinned man. And over the years they became the parents of eleven children.

I sometimes lay in bed thinking that I considered my father a genius, partly because I am prejudiced and partly because I was told by many of his teachers that he was the smartest person that they had ever taught. Daddy was biracial; he had fourteen siblings ; his father *was* a white man with blond hair and blue eyes—a Methodist preacher; my father's mother, who was born in Lenoir, North Carolina, was part Native American/ Lumbee Indian. She had reddish tone olive skin, and her long, thick silky braids hung down to her waistline. For some reason or another, Daddy never told us about his family background or his heritage. I'm not sure if it was because of shame or what. He mostly told me. Don't be talking and writing about what you don't know about. So I never knew who my grandfather's parents were.

Daddy attended Shaw University, unfortunately he never graduated, first because he was sent to fight in the Philippines during World War II, and second because his family became too large.

So after coming home from the Army, the twelve to sixteen hours a day work schedule, left no time for his schooling.

I was two years old and, Ruth, my oldest sister was four when my father returned home from the Army. And before he had to work three jobs, Daddy taught Ruth a lot of French words and the Lord's Prayer in French. Mama said I was too little to learn, but I listen real good and learned it anyway, I suppose this was the *first real evidence of my determination*. So at age six when I went to school, I can remember the pleasure it gave me to say "Bonjour, Madam," each morning to my first grade teacher.

****

I packed our clothes, readied the three babies, Raven was two, Pricilla was one. I don't know how I managed to do it, but I hailed a taxicab on the street that took us down to the bus station in Washington, DC. As I sat there with Dawn on my lap, Raven and Priscilla stood nearby—poor little things. Pricilla had not been walking long. While we waited for the bus, there was an ashtray with white sand inside. Pricilla kept putting her hand and grabbing the white sand—I had to keep pulling her away. The bus station was extremely crowded and there was no place for Raven and Pricilla to sit. My heart sank as I looked up into the eyes of Walter who had come to take the children and me back to our one room. He had no money for rent, and therefore; the room was no longer available. I'm not exactly sure of how we learned of Travelers Aid Society, but the five of us had to go there for help. They secured a room in a hotel until a place to stay could be found again.

Once again a room was found at the Moore's home in Washington for the five of us. Walter found work again at the Pontiac car dealership where the professional boxer, Bobby Foster worked. But again this did not last. I had to return home with the children. And Walter soon followed. The five of us lived with Walter's parents and two sisters again until he found work in Morristown.

****

This time, Walter found a job at the local Morristown bakery. He frequented a local club that was located down the hill from his parents' home on Morgan Mill Road—the Green Light Inn. It usually stayed open until the wee hours of the morning.

Occasionally, he would take me to the club with him. There we would sometimes meet with some of Walter's high school buddies—guys he grew up with in Morristown. His friends love being around the two of us.

At the Green Light Inn, on this particular night, Walter joined Jake, an old school buddy and his girlfriend, Fanny. Fanny was carrying Jake's baby, and they were having an argument. But when we joined them the argument subsided for a time.

We were all drinking shots of cheap Bourbon; Walter and Jake were quite intoxicated at the time and Jake complimented me. "You sure are a pretty girl, Emily."

Fanny's chest swelled with jealous rage. "What do you want that bitch at this table for?"

Walter became angry. "You had better shut that whore up Jake." He threatened. "Or you're going to have to kick my ass." Jake said something in defiance.

Walter took a swing with his fist at Jake. The owner of the club came over and insisted that they should take that argument outside. Walter grabbed Jake in the collar almost dragging him out of the door. Fanny began to beat Walter from the back. I started to pull Fanny off of Walter. Fanny whipped out a knife.

In an instant, I felt blood flowing from somewhere. Someone came to get me. A kind voice said, "You need to get to the hospital, you've been cut." When I came to realize what had happened to me, I lay on a table at Union Memorial Hospital. The doctor was stitching me up. I had been sliced during the fight.

The next morning when I awoke, I forced myself to look into the mirror. Huge bandages covered these wounds that had been stitched at the hospital. My God, I questioned, how could this have happened? I thought here I was following in behind Walter, and now his habits are my misfortune. I've always heard that a drunk will wreck the car and kill everybody in the automobile and then get up and walk away from it all. I wept quietly to think of the night before. I had been hurt—but Walter was fine.

When God bestowed the gift of humility and beauty upon a female, she has enemies unsuspectingly. I never suspected Fanny as my enemy—not in a million years. We were not bosom buddies or anything like that, but I had never done anything for her to try to destroy me. Through this unfortunate pain, I had to come to terms with this vital lesson—to be aware of female jealousy.

The bandages were removed within a short time; there had been only thin marks on my body. The old saying—God takes care of babies and fools—I had been both—and God had been kind. I had no business whatsoever at that club with Walter—I had no business indulging in drinking with him; I was only a child of sixteen with adult responsibilities. When I think back to what could have happened to me under the circumstances, I have to ask what was I thinking—*I just didn't know any better*. It's difficult to hold a child accountable for poor decisions before the development of the frontal lobe in the brain?

Part IX
Escalated Violence

*W*alter had moved us into a house on First
Street in Bright Town, and I spent most of my days
sewing curtains to fix the house up, cleaning, cooking
and swatting roaches; changing diapers in between
fights with Walter which caused black eyes and bruised
lips.   Once my mother asked, "What in the world
happened to your face?

Inside her heart and mind, Mama had to know
that the bruises were not the results of splattered grease,
as I had told her. I was too ashamed to tell her the truth.
That Walter had done that to me—beaten me about the
head and face.

The police in Morristown told me, **"JUST KILL
HIM.   NOTHING WILL HAPPEN TO YOU!"**
Before he moved us into the house, Walter had woken
up one morning and put a loaded gun to my temple just
for fun—just because he could do that to me, as I sat at
the kitchen table at his parents' home. I bolted, out of
fright for my life, out of the kitchen door and ran to a
neighbor's house and called the police. I knew I could
never kill anyone. I signed a police report and later
dropped the charges.

The policeman who told me to kill Walter
certainly had his motives—as he stood there in Mrs.
Phifer's living room to take the report the morning

Walter held the gun to my head, he looked around and then asked me if he could come and spend time with me because he said, "I've always liked you." I told my mother-in-law, Mrs. Phifer, the very day it happened. I could tell her anything.   But like any mother, nevertheless, even she knew Walter had a mental problem, but she did not want her son put behind bars by me—even though he was crazy as hell and deserved it.

One night when Walter came home about two o'clock in the morning, he climbed into bed and faced the wall, and I could smell the alcohol oozing from his pours. I had not seen him since he left home for work early the morning before. I touched his back and asked him where he had been. He turned over and hit me on the collar bone instantly cracking it. Excruciating pain went down my neck and my arm. I couldn't move my head or my arm. I started to sob and scrambled out of bed holding my chin close to my shoulder where I had received the blow-- holding onto my right arm with my left hand. I managed somehow to get dressed and walked down the hill to my parents' house in the middle of the night. When I arrived at the porch of Mom and Dad's house, I could not go inside. I just stood there outside, sobbing and ashamed of being hurt—hoping someone inside would discover me standing there.   I turned and walked back up the street and up the hill to the Phifer's. When I returned, I managed to knock on Mrs. Phifer's bedroom door. She instantly opened the door and rushed out when she saw my condition.

"Oh no—oh no!" She exclaimed. As she dressed, she went to where Walter lay in bed. "What in the world did you hit that girl for, Walter?" There was no response. Mrs. Phifer called a taxicab and when it arrived, she took me to Dr. Clegg's house. She left me there in the taxi for a short while and went inside, she returned to the taxi and the driver followed Dr. Clegg's car to his uptown office in Morristown. Ironically, it was the same office where the "good doctor" had molested me two years earlier at age fifteen.

After Walter fractured my clavicle and the bandages were removed, there was a deep crack in my shoulder blade that has never completely healed and changed.

I knew I had to get away—to save my own life. I answered an ad in the newspaper advertising jobs for maids in the North. I soon left my poor little children in the care of my daddy's sister, Aunt Loving who moved into the house, and I left Morristown on the Greyhound bus seeking a job as a mother's helper in New York.

It didn't take long before I was hired to work in Delmar, New Jersey with a Jewish family—in fact I was hired the same day that I arrived at the agency. A set of Jewish male twins were married to a set of Jewish female twins and each had three children. I later learned that the husbands were in the insurance business in the downtown area of Delmar; the wives did not work outside the home. I was hired to work in the household of one of the families, Unice and Ervin Klontz as a mother's helper.

On the day I was hired, I remember having to fill out a long questionnaire at the New York City Domestic Agency. Then I sat waiting among a large group of young black women hoping to find jobs. A white man in a blue suit came up and directed me to follow him. I went into his office, and Unice, a middle-aged sophisticated looking, well dressed Jewish female stood there with her sister and three young boys; she held my form in her hand. They looked me over from head to toe like an apple they were going to bite; Unice introduced herself, her sister, and her children—the three boys, Bobby, Warren and Ervin Jr. Then Unice asked me several questions including my name and if I liked children. I sensed she just wanted to hear me speak, because my name was on the questionnaire, and I had stated that I liked children. The next thing I remember about that day is putting my bag into the trunk of a white convertible Mustang and speeding over the George Washington Bridge from New York to New Jersey with Unice behind the wheel. Her sister sat beside her, and I sat in the back seat with Unice's three children with our hair blowing in the wind.

I thought I could make money and send it back to Morristown. For three months, I worked in Unice and Ervin's spacious, tri-level three bedrooms home. There wasn't much to do that I wasn't accustomed to doing, except it was just easier—set out the cereal for breakfast in the morning. And after the boys left to walk to school, I loaded the dishwasher, used the washer and dryer to launder the clothes, change and make the beds, —easy work like that. Unice did all of the shopping and cooking. Occasionally, when she went shopping, she took me with her to the mall in Delmar.

My living space was a huge room between the upstairs and the basement—a room with large windows, oil paintings on the walls and shelves filled with books; a table with a radio and sofa set in a corner. During the day Unice would be gone shopping or out with her sister, so after my chores, I played the radio and did the "Twist" in my room to "Do you Love Me" by Berry Gordy. I washed, straightened and set my hair. I remember asking Unice's permission to use the kitchen stove to heat the straightening comb to press my hair. Of course she agreed. "Yes. None of the other girls that worked here could do their own hair." She said. I sometimes tried my hand at playing "Chopsticks" on the baby grand piano that sat in the living room or I read.

The first book I ever read was in Delmar, chosen from the collection of books on the shelves in my living space, *The Enchanted Cup,* a thick book by Dorothy James Roberts. I was determined to read.

In such a short period of time, I learned so much from Unice about Jewish foods being kosher, dietary laws ritually pure. I learned how to make meatballs and spaghetti, baked chicken drizzled with Westchester sauce and soy sauce, fried Cod, which she prepared every Friday by dipping it in egg and flour before frying it. She heated and served can green beans without any seasoning. And when I complained about her not using any butter or salt and pepper to season the can green beans, she chuckled and told me, "You won't make a very good little Jewish girl. I never asked her what she meant by that. I just figured she meant that they didn't use much butter, salt and pepper.

My main responsibility was to prepare Ervin's soup before he ate his dinner on Monday evenings, because Unice had decided to return to college. And I had to be there with the boys when Unice and Ervin got all dressed up to go out clubbing on every Wednesday night. Bobby the oldest boy seemed to be closer to his mother than the other two boys always complained. "You're always going out." He would say. I supposed he was at the Oedipal Stage—the Oedipus complex in Greek mythology referring to a son's love for his mother at a certain age.

The boys were wonderful children who showered and retired to their rooms to watch television each night after dinner. They were usually in bed each school night by ten. On Saturdays the family attended the Jewish Center for religious purposes. On some Saturdays I played Gin Rummy with Warren, the youngest boy, who whined each time I won. Finally, Unice asked me to allow him to win sometimes, which made him so happy.

Sunday was my payday and my off day. Delmar was a little over a two- hour's bus ride from Patterson where Uncle Hector still lived. After my first two weeks in Delmar, I telephoned my uncle and told him I would take the bus to visit him if he would drive me back to Delmar. He agreed, and after my first visit he started coming to Delmar to pick me up in his   latest model 1961, red, Buick Electra 225 at least twice a month and take me to Patterson to his girlfriend's house for a good hot soul-food meal.

As a mother's helper in Delmar, I felt freer and safer than I had ever felt in my youth. It was easy to avoid thinking and dwelling on the earlier negative experiences of before when Walter and I lived there.

But eventually, I knew I could not stay away; although I was only a child of seventeen myself, I had to resume the responsibility as the mother of my three children, although by then I was only seventeen years old. On the day I left Delmar, Uncle Hector came to pick me up, and I said my good-byes to the Klontz' and their boys.

****

When I returned to Morristown Walter had moved in again with his parents with the children. And by age eighteen years old I discovered I was about to have another child in the fall. Carrie was born in September. At age two, I was hired at Allen Overall, a sewing factory in downtown Morristown that made Army jackets.

And when she became four, in December I did as I had so many times before. I made the trip—an East to West odyssey this time with four children. But this trip would make all the difference in the world. This trip represented a brand new life. I imagined educational opportunities for myself that my family could never provide. I had learned that as a two year resident of California, one can attend a junior college for free.

As I sat on the train with my children anticipating the three- day trip to California, I thought of Walter *having* to leave Morristown. He had done what he called "defended my honor" and was standing a good chance of being sent to prison.

I thought of how it all came about. I had visited my parents one evening and was walking home after dark up the hill to the where we lived with Walter's parents. I wore white shorts and a yellow blouse. A car speeded around the curve. Most of us are familiar with the circumstances under which little old men after dark crave for little young black girls in the 60s. As the car sped around the curve, I ran up the hill to home.

Walter was standing on the corner of the street where we lived. No doubt spying on me—if Larry was anywhere in Morristown, I would have hell to pay. He would call Larry's parents' home and threaten to kill him. I don't doubt that both times when he held a gun to my head and when he broke my collar bone it had something to do with Larry being in town.

While he stood on the corner of the street, the car driven by a middle-aged man stopped to ask Walter,

"Did you see a girl walk by here wearing white shorts?" Realizing that this man was speaking of me outraged Walter and he replied, "Yeah, I saw her; I'll take you to her!"

The man unlocked the car door and motioned for Walter to climb in.   Walter now breathing with excitement asked, "What did you say the girl was wearing?"

"She had on a pair of white shorts. She was a little red, big butt girl. I thought she came up the street there."

Walter found it hard to contain himself; all the images, he said, of racial injustices rushed through his mind, Walter clenched his teeth and fists.

The man repeated, "I thought she came up that street, there." The man was flush red and anxious. His eyes stretched as he drove he looked from the road to Walter and back to the road again.

"I know where she lives and I'll take you to her."

The man looked at Walter excitedly, asked, "Do you know her?"

"Yeah, turn here and go down in Ebb Town and I'll get my partner so he can go to the house with me."

The man started turned the car and drove off again. They stopped at Henry's house and picked him up. Walter directed the man to drive the car to a dark secluded part of Morristown.

"Yeah, this is where she lives." Walter's eyes were wide and filled with anger—"Stop the car!" He yelled.

"Where's the house? The man questioned. "Will you go and get her?" The little flush man questioned curiously.

Walter's eyes widened with more anger. "Right down there!" When the car stopped, he opened the door and got out and went around to the driver's side where the man sat. He opened his door.

"Hey, what are you doin' boy? He yelled to Walter.

"Boy?" "Boy?" Walter dragged the man out and began to hit him again and again until he bled. Henry took his wallet and removed his money. They left the man there and ran away.

The next day the police came and questioned Mrs. Phifer to find out if Walter had anything to do with—or if she knew anything about a white man getting attacked and robbed by two young black men in Ebb Town the night before..   The tall, huge, white policeman stood in the living room of Mrs. Phifer's home and told her, "The man told us that one of the attackers was a tall, slim black man in his twenties who was standing on your street, and the other one was a short black man of about the same age." Mrs. Phifer of course assured the police that her son had nothing to do with the attack.

So Walter had to cut a low profile after the incident. He figured the police was going to be watching him. He couldn't hide out at Jake's. After the fight with him at the Blue Light In, he severed his ties. Walter had to get out of town quick. He knew the authorities wouldn't stand for a black man harming a white man no matter what the little man's alleged intentions were. Five days later, Walter used his check from the bakery and boarded the next flight rolling out of Morristown headed for California to escape possible imprisonment. He said he could find work because he had an older cousin employed by the city.   Henry went to California with him.

****

In California, Walter found a job working at the McCulloch Corporation in Culver City where, he said, outboard motors were made; he cleaned up the stations once the pieces had been assembled and put together. In his letters to me, he said he was making really good money-- much more than any job in Morristown. But he never sent me any because he said he was saving it up for when the children and I arrived.

Walter and his cousin Sam met the children and me in a convertible at the Los Angeles train station on Alameda Street. He had taken an apartment in a building in Los Angeles on Vermont Avenue at 54th. On the way there from Alameda Street toward North Los Angeles Street, Sam merged the convertible onto the 101 toward Hollywood and then to the Harbor Freeway. We were soon on the 110 toward Exit 19A toward 51 Street.

As the children and I sat in the back seat I took in the essence of the landscape--tall palm trees seemingly to touch bright blue skies, and wide freeway lanes with fancy speeding cars, the breath-taking beauty was like a dream—the girls, Raven, Pricilla, Dawn and Carrie were quiet and seemed to be at awe of it all, with the wind blowing in our hair, and the sun on our faces, Sam pulled the car into a parking space on Vermont Avenue directly in front of the apartment intersecting 54th Street. The weather was hot and fine.

I later learned that the area was convenient to everything, near-by schools in walking distance, churches, the Rapid Transit District bus line, local shops and the grocery store. The apartment was located directly over a barbeque restaurant.

After we settled into the small two bedroom apartment, the first thing was to get the children enrolled into Bud Long Avenue Elementary School. Now I could seek out the sewing factories in Los Angeles to use the power sewing machine skills learned at Allen Overall. I could work while the children were in school during the day. By then the girls were ages, four, six, seven and eight—I was twenty-three, and Walter was twenty-seven.

My private dreams were to return to school so that I could fulfill my ambition to become a teacher. At first, I managed to get a job working close to home, in walking distance at Wise Department Store, on Vermont Avenue and then, I seek out the local adult night school. I could take the RTD across the street from the apartment on Vermont and ride to Manual Arts High School. I could attend two or three nights a week, once the children were home from school.

Walter's sister, Lizzie, who was the same age as I, had come to California shortly after graduating from high school, worked in Los Angeles; she had been living with their cousin, Sam and his wife in Los Angeles. She decided to come and live with us, and she thoughtfully agreed to watch the children while I attended night school. I thought the arrangement would be perfect. I had great plans.

Attending Manual Arts High was like a dream. My English teacher and the classmates revealed such admiration for me. I could "ace" any test in English. When there was something special to do like presenting the instructor with a birthday card from the students, I was chosen for the role.   I was so shy then, so inexperienced when it came to expressing myself, that on the night I presented the card, I could hardly manage to get the words to come out of my mouth.   Besides being smart, I believe the only other reason I was chosen was that I was pretty—that's all, I later discovered that I had been totally unaware of how others, especially my classmates reacted to my beauty.   This awareness did not occur to me until much later in life.

One afternoon on my way to Manual Arts, I met this girl named Thelma at the bus stop on Vermont. She was a single mother of a pretty little one-year old girl, who she brought over to show her off as soon as I told her where I lived. Thelma lived with her sisters two streets over in a huge house on 52nd Street; our acquaintance eventually developed into a lifelong friendship.   I didn't have any other friends, the ones that develop while you're in school because I married during my high school freshman year.   I had five sisters and five brothers, and they were close to each other—but they were not close to me.   Basically, they did not know me beyond age fourteen.

Lizzie lived with us, shared the expenses of the household—she was a great person, but for some reason she was distant.   She was close to Sam, his friends and her mother, Mrs. Phifer and her sister back home in Morristown. Now that I think about it, perhaps it was that she was ashamed of her brother, but like me—I believe she was afraid of him also. I had seen him "pounce" on her once while we lived in Morristown at their parents' for no apparent reason; except for something she said that he took offense to.   And the two of us had witnessed him fight his own father, Mr. Phifer, when he told Walter, one night, "You need to get off your mother's back; stop running around in the streets and spending your mama's money." Walter hit him in the mouth—they nearly tore the place apart. I supposed Walter protested against his father's advice, when he was simply following in his own father's footsteps. The fight with his father was a testament to his insanity. What son would attack his own father for giving him some advice—only a lunatic. Anyway, there I was without any relative on the West Coast--I was happy to have Thelma, so she and I became as close as any two sisters could be.

The plan for school and job in Los Angeles festered and kept festering. The big city of Los Angeles offered a bigger opportunity for Walter to be irresponsible and dangerous—his bad habits magnified—running around with Henry, who had also gotten an apartment in Los Angeles, and staying out late—I'm sure with other women, drinking, spending all of his money—never adequately providing for his family. Their school clothes and necessities had been provided for them while I worked at the Allen Overall's sewing factory, at Cooks Canteen, and as a cook at the dingy Blue Light Inn all in Morristown.

One day I came home and there was this funny smell in the apartment coming from the kitchen. I opened the oven door and this green grass looking stuff was inside. I discovered him cooking hashish in the oven. I blew my top—I told Walter, "We have children to raise, and you're bringing some illegal substances here. Don't ever let me discover you doing something in this apartment again or I will call the police on you." My words and tone shocked Walter. He immediately took the stuff out of the stove and out of the apartment. Now that I think about it, I supposed he was smoking dope *and* drinking alcohol during the 60s. I was just a naïve girl from "the country." I just didn't know nor was I exposed to anything. My only experience was being married being pregnant and having babies—and I was still a virgin. I don't ever remember knowing what I know now about having a climax during sex and I was twenty-three years old.

I finally learned that there was birth control after I had four children by age nineteen. After my fourth child, was born, before relocating to California, one day I had an epiphany and asked Dr. Perry, the local black doctor in Morristown, how could I stop getting pregnant—he told me about birth control pills. I learned from the doctor that white women had birth control pills thirty years before black women did. Anyway, once I had this knowledge, in Morristown, I scrambled "like crazy" getting the money to pay for the pills when it was time. When I say scramble I mean gathering up pennies, nickels, and dimes and then taking Mr. Albert's taxi cab uptown to Wilson's drug store. In California, I could walk to the drugstore. I vowed that no man would ever get another baby in this body.

After living in Los Angeles for two months, Walter lost his job at the McCulloch Corporation. There wasn't much time in between him finding other employment, this time an office job in another city in California—at the Watts Manufacturing Company in Compton. And as usual, he wanted to move the family to Compton near the job. I had no choice but to pull the children out of school, and we all moved to Compton, a residential suburbs on the south side in California. His sister moved in again with Sam and his wife.

A tiger cannot change his stripes—Walter, could not change his habits either, not even if his life depended on it. It was the same old story, the same old scene. When I complained, he struck me and said, "I'll kill you." He told me, "I can see that cheating grin on your face." This is the way it was: If I stayed home, I was waiting for someone—if I went to the grocery store—on the bus mind you—I was meeting someone.

Even a little shy girl can only take so much—I just got fed up, so I bit the bullet, one morning I told Walter that we needed to talk about something. I had fed the children their breakfast and sent them to watch cartoons on television. Walter and I sat at the kitchen table across from each other. I said in my timid voice because I was scared, "Walter, I need to talk to you about something."

"What is it? He asked immediately, with an extremely mean and intimidating expression on his face. I suppose inside he knew he had to face reality—it's not like he didn't know this was eventually coming—I was more mature—I had tested my wings at Manual Arts—I liked what I experienced there getting an education—in the company with people who did not try to intimidate or violate or harm me. I wanted to acclimate into this part of society—make something of myself. Besides, by then I learned that once I lived in California for two years, as a
resident, I could attend the junior college for free.—I *wanted this desperately.*

"Walter, it seems that we just can't get along". I continued. "Why don't we separate for a while until we can get ourselves together—figure out what we want?"

He was staring at me from across the table. "Yeah," he whispered—his alter-ego manifesting—

"You can *sep-a-rate,* and when I find you," he threatened. "I'll cut off your legs and arms, and pull the hairs off my p----, and leave you somewhere to die slowly." Obviously Walter had snapped and gone over to his violent and unstable personality. He banged his fist "Boom!"--down hard on the table and sprang up like a wild animal. He leaped toward me. "I'll just kill you now!" He grabbed me by the throat and pulled me from the chair before I had time to run, forcing me to the floor. He was over me piercing his thumbs into and squeezing my neck simultaneously. I couldn't breathe. I screamed, "No-no! Help me! Oh God, oh God."

Walter pressed harder with his hands around my throat—"Yeah, oh God," He said as he squeezed harder.

I felt life leaving me. It started to get dark. My body began to jerk; I kept kicking my legs—scrambling to live—trying to pull his hands from around my neck. I was no match for the six foot two man.

Partly conscious, I heard my poor little children screaming, **"Daddy no! No!"** My babies saved my life that day. I still shudder to think that I would have died on that kitchen floor in Compton that morning if it were not for their angelic voices causing Walter to snap back to reality.

When I regained total consciousness, my four children, Raven, Pricilla, Dawn and Carrie were on their knees leaning over me. Walter stood near the kitchen sink. My neck and nose were bleeding. I scrambled up weakly, from the floor. I asked Walter to take me to the doctor. He seemed to be back to the good Walter now— he reluctantly agreed to take me to the hospital. He told the children to go to their room and they obeyed I'm sure out of fear of him. He walked to the kitchen back door to wait for me while I dressed. I ran out of the front door. I don't remember exactly, but I believe to a telephone booth down the street, or to a neighbor's house, and call the police. I didn't realize I needed medical attention.

Now looking back and finally researching strangulation, I learned: Nearly three in four survivors in a study by the Maine Coalition to End Domestic Violence did not seek medical attention after being strangled, perhaps out of fear of exposing the abuse or not realizing that without proper medical care, strangulation can lead to death days or even weeks after the attack.

Ironically, when the police arrived, the officer informed me, "Lady, the only thing we can do is to wait with you while you pack a bag to leave the house to go and stay somewhere else." I packed a bag—I wanted to take my children with me--Walter refused to allow me to take them—I had to leave them with this animal. I took the city bus back to Los Angeles, to Thelma's.

I befriended a retired school teacher whose husband was a retired Los Angeles attorney. The couple lived around the corner from Thelma. The Neusome's owned a beautiful and spacious home on 52 and Bud Long Avenue. They owned duplex houses in the neighborhood that they rented out. I saw a for rent sign in the window one day in passing. Upon seeking an apartment to rent—and hearing my story—my predicament, Mrs. Neusome responded, "Well as pretty as you are, you don't need an apartment all by yourself; you can stay right here with my husband and me."

The empathetic couple allowed me to stay there while I found work in a sewing factory in the downtown area of Los Angeles that made the same Army jacket made in the sewing factory in Morristown—of course this company paid more money. I was able to use the skills I had trained for back in Morristown.

Following the violent attack when Walter tried to kill me in Compton, and I had to leave my children, I did managed to get them back. I took the children to the Neusome's when I stole them from Walter.

My girlfriend Thelma, Mrs. Neusome, and a male student from Manual Art's night school where all instrumental in the success of my plan. This student drove me to Compton, to help with the kidnapping of my children from their father and his white girlfriend. I remember waiting in the car across the street that night from where my children lived with their father and this woman.   I watched the two of them leave before I sneaked in and kidnapped them from him.

When I did get the children, I took them to the Neusomes' home, a well-lighted place; their little heavenly brown faces gleamed to see me, their hands reached for me and their feet showed almost as black as tar. It seemed that they hadn't been bathed in a month of Sundays.   Their skinny bodies starved for nourishment, motherly love and soap and water.

****

Not long after reenrolling the children in Bud Long Avenue Elementary School, it was about this time that I rounded the corner at the Neusome's, after getting off from work, I discovered Walter standing there beside Thelma in front of the Neusome's home.

"I've come for you and the kids," He said, standing there in a suit, and managing to look pitiful. "I'm *not* leaving here without you."

I wanted to "ball", scream, run and hide, but it was too late. I questioned, "How did you find me?"

"Thelma told me where you were--I mean Thelma's *sister* told me where you were. I love you, Emily, and I want you and the kids to come home—and I'm *taking* you and the kids with me." Within a week, Walter, the children and I were back together in an apartment he rented in a two-story apartment building, this time on 54th Street in Los Angeles. Lizzie soon moved in with us again.

One Saturday early afternoon Lizzie and I were rounding the corner going shopping on Vermont Avenue. We experienced the surprise of a lifetime. A man standing on the corner said to us, "I think the police have your friend in the bank." There were several police cars in front of the bank. Walter had been caught inside the corner bank. He had forced entrance—they took him away in handcuffs. He was later charged with attempted robbery and two counts of forgery. The courts found him guilty and sent him to Soledad State Prison in California for two years.

While Walter was imprisoned, I continue to work and care for the children as best I could. Lizzie continued to live with me. Not long after he was sent away, I was accompanied by a friend of his and Lizzie's to make the long and tiring journey on the Monterey-Salinas Transit line 23 to visit him at Soledad. He sat there behind bars veering cruelly at me with his lips squeezed tightly together and threatened me, "You know I'm going to kill you when I get out of here, don't you?"

I can't even begin to remember, or begin to explain how shocked I was and how hurt I felt at the time.

I decided that very day to file for a divorce while he was behind bars. It wasn't a cruel thing to do—it was the only way to escape from him. I learned that his imprisonment allowed me incontestable grounds for a divorce.

I befriended the next door neighbor, Mike, on 54th street who had relatives living in the San Fernando Valley who owned a house they wanted to rent—I needed desperately to get my children and myself away from Los Angeles. I figured we could hide in the Valley, so the children and I, with Mike's assistance, moved in 1970 to the Valley on Vaughn Street into a small two bedroom house with a huge backyard where the girls could play.

Having no income with the father of my children incarcerated, when I moved to the Valley; I was entitled to Welfare—as a mother of four with no family or monetary assistance. The children enrolled into the local school—Fillmore Street School in Lake View Terrace, California. The transition from Los Angeles to the Valley didn't seem to affect them considering what they had been through—poor little babies. They were good and obedient children—I'm sure they understood my intensions for them.

The transition had been a beneficial one for me too. I attended Adult School at Central City, and then later obtained a Certificate in Secretarial Science and Stenography. I found a job as a secretary and paste-up girl at the local newspaper, the Record Ledger in Tujunga.

Two years later when Walter was released from prison—he found us in the Valley and came to the house while I was at work. He knocked on the door, and said—"Open the door." Raven opened the door and he stood there. He told our children, "Tell your mama I'll be back, and when I do, I'm going to kill all of you!" Then the coward left. Imagine telling your four little innocent children something that horrifying.

Raven call me at work understandably terrified, she said "Mommy, Daddy came here and told us he was going to kill us all." I didn't tell anyone on my job about my problem, except that I had a family emergency and needed to leave work. I left work in my Volkswagen. Driving down Foothill Boulevard to home, tears from terror rolled down my cheeks into my blouse. I had no idea how this would unfold. A Cell phone would have been a convenient commodity; however they didn't exist in the 70s, so it was necessary to wait and make calls for help when I arrived home. The drive took approximately twenty to thirty minutes. I prayed and dried my tear—I had to console my children and be strong for them. When I opened the door to the house—they ran to me. They could tell I had been crying—"Mommy," They said, "Don't worry." as they held on to me—as we held on to each other.

I recalled what the police had told me about doing nothing when Walter tried to kill me in Compton. So this time I didn't bother calling them. I call six foot four Mike, who had moved from Los Angeles, and now residing with his six foot six professor cousin, Ben, in a house in the Valley. Basically, *one* of my motives for befriending him was that he was a gentle giant. I knew he liked me well enough to protect me. He had listened patiently, and wiped my tears many nights when I cried and shared with him the stories of how Walter abused me over the years. Mike and Ben immediately came to my rescue. Mike instructed me to telephone Walter and keep him on the telephone until they arrived at the apartment where he lived with Lizzie in Los Angeles. Lizzie and a cousin who moved to California from Morristown lived together. Her cousin had a dog, so when I heard the dog barking, I believed Mike and Ben had apparently arrived at their apartment.

It was told to me that when Walter opened the door, he was staring down the barrel of a shotgun. He was told "If you harm Emily, you can get hurt too. So don't bother her and her children again, or you will regret it—so just leave them alone and go on with your life—IT'S OVER!."

I remembered the police in Morristown's words-- "Just kill Him and Nothing Will Happen to You! But I knew I could never kill anyone. This was not a part of my cultural background. My parents had taught us you will be punished for wrongdoings—but killing someone was totally out of the question. And I don't think any of us, Mike, Ben nor I believed in taking the law into our own hands—but what were we to do, to keep this maniac—this psychopath from killing all of us?

Later, when the telephone rang it was Walter on the other end. "Yeah, that was real smart," He said, "I didn't realize I could get hurt too."

My response was, "I WOULD RATHER BE *DEAD* THAN TO LIVE WITH YOU!"

Ironically, Walter never threatened me or the children again. So it seems, he wasn't as crazy as I suspected.

Children have great resiliency. Each time my daughters experienced a negative interruption in our lives or observed something painful happening to me, they didn't completely fall apart. *They kept it together* by rallied around me trying to be as strong as their little selves could be—bless their little hearts. They had me; they had each other.   And when a crisis in our lives came to an end, they didn't sit around crying and whining or blaming anyone—asking what if?   Once we prayed about it, took a good shower, and I cooked and fed them a good meal, they didn't worry about the past; they bounced right back to their happy, playful, loving and successful selves—attending school, participating in the Gifted and Talent Programs, learning to swim, attending church, attending stage plays at theaters with me, and hanging out with the drama team—writing and acting in school plays. But, I never really saw or realized how the destructive repercussions of the abuse would affect our lives and the extent the harm had done to them or to me until many years later in our lives. I suppose these are the misconceptions of youth elasticity for both my children and me.

I buried myself in an endeavor to be a role model for my children and myself by matriculating through education. From Secretarial Science, I learned to get a well paying job; one must get a good education.   **I became *unstoppable for getting a degree to change our lives—to make it better for my children and myself.   Ironically, I came to the unbelievable realization that I was without a doubt a favored child, especially with all that we had been through; I asked myself—what else can possibly happen?***

So for the next two years I cared for my children needs while I worked a part-time job at Filmore Street School as a Special Education assistant, and I attended college as an English major three afternoons a week, Monday, Wednesday and Thursday, carrying a full load (twelve units).   On many nights after grocery shopping, preparing dinner, seeing after the children's needs, it was necessary for me to stay up the rest of the night to complete the writing of an English paper or study for an exam, jump up, shower, drink a cup of coffee, drive the Volkswagen to campus and knock the bottom out of an English test. I was among the top third in my classes, a Dean's List Student; invited to join Tia Alpha Epsilon and surprisingly, I was usually the only black student in my English class.

One of my old English professors, the late Dr George Herrick saw to it that as a little black girl on campus, I was exposed to academia—such as scholarships, grants, organizations. He showed favor because I made A's in his English class. Many years later, when I wrote to him revealing my intentions to write a book, he was so happy and agreed to read it. When he passed, approximately twenty years ago, his wife wrote and told me of the unfortunate news. I felt the lost a great friend.

When school was out, during the summer I worked a full-time job. Safeco Title Insurance Company on Burbank Boulevard hired me in the Payoff Department working with the Title Officers, who has the role of an attorney when commercial or personal property was purchased through the company. I was using computers for land title searches in the 70s as a part of my job. At the end of the summer I returned to college. Two years later, I earned an English degree from Cal State University, at Northridge.

Part X
The Breakdown

Shortly before graduation from California
State University at Northridge, Larry, of all people
wrote a letter to me. **It was 1:30 pm when the first
letter came, September 11, 1977.** It read:

Dear Emily,

I know you are surprised to be getting a
letter from me. Especially after all these years! I don't
know if you are married or living with anyone, or what.
I just hope my writing doesn't cause you any problems
between you, and your man. (Smile).

Anyway, I feel that what I have to say will come
as some shock to you. I don't know really where to
start. First let me start by bringing you up-to-date with
me. Maybe then you can somewhat understand how I
came to end up in a place like this...

It all started back long ago when I was small, and
got a sax one Christmas. At first it was just a toy to me,
but after a while I found that I really like the "moans"
and groaning like sounds that came from the horn.
That's what really made me want to get into it.

I learned all that I could there in Morristown, so I
went off to school (A&T) to learn more about the
instrument. It didn't take me long to know that was not
what I was looking for. All they wanted to do was give

me a B.S. degree in music so I could come out, and march a high school band up and down the streets. So I played around in clubs until I got a job in the Joe Tex band, and went on the road. I really thought I was doing something <u>great</u>! I thought I was into the big times. I left him, and even got with bigger names artists!!!

All hell broke loose when I got with the Aretha Franklin show. It was in the late 60s when she first came out with "Respect." At that time, she was about the hottest thing in the country. It was the first time I had ever played in an all-star band.

Most of the guys in the band were on dope. By my just getting out there, I was ready to try <u>anything</u>. I tried some just to see what it was like. I knew then that I was going to get hooked, because I liked it too much. When I got high I felt as if there was nothing that I couldn't play. I played, and stayed high!

I played and played until I was one of the most talked about horn players on the road. I stayed with Aretha Franklin until Dr. Martin Luther King was killed, and all the shows were cancelled. The band was out of a job, so the union called us back to New York where we went into the Apollo Theater, as the house band.

I don't know what happened much after that. Now it all seems like a bad dream. All I know is that I stayed high most of the time. I kept on using more and more drugs until I couldn't keep up my habit on what money I made in the theater. That's when I went to doing other things.

I did anything that I could do to get more for dope!!! And <u>I mean anything!</u>

I went from selling dope to pimping whores to keep up my habit. Things really got bad. I lost my job.

I even pawned the only thing that I owned at the time—
MY HORN!

One night I was caught in a raid, and went to jail.
After I was in jail for about two weeks the union man
came and talked to me. He told me that this girl had
been to him, and talked to him about me. Anyway, he
told me that if I promised to let the junk go, then he
would bail me out, and put me back to work.

Well, when I got out Sam and Dave was getting a
package show together along with some other artists
whom I don't remember. Anyway, this girl had gotten
my horn back for me, and I was back on the stage
playing again. I stayed clean for a while, but after a
while I was back on the junk. The whole time we were
on the road, I would always slip away from the others
and find some place to buy some dope. By the time the
tour was on its last night, I was strung out again.

The show closed down in Texas. The band went
into a club, as a house band until the office got another
show together. That's where I went down for my last
time. After a while I lost my job again. I would get out
of one jail only to go into another. I stopped playing all
together.

Anyway, it got so bad that I couldn't play if I
wanted to. At that point the only thing that I could get to
come out of my horn was the blues. No one wants to
hear the low down blues all the time. So I just let it go.
The last time I got into something I just gave up and
came back home to Morristown to try to get things
together.

That didn't work either. It was not long before I
got into some trouble down here. This time I got three
to five years for buying, and selling hot goods. I stayed

in for around fifteen months, and made parole. Now I'm back for breaking parole, even though I was out around Christmas. I know you are wondering why in the hell am I writing, and telling you all this shit.

Well it's like this. Emily since I have seen you, I have had and been through many women, some of them were good women, and some not so good. But I have never forgotten about you. You were my first real love, and my only real love. Even now when I am at home, I still go out there into the old school yard late at night, and think and relive all the times we spent there together. I always keep up on what you are doing.

I know you are into some very good things out there. That's one reason why I never tried to get in touch with you. Many times I have been within a few miles from where you live, but I could never bring myself to come to see you. A friend of mine stays not too far from you. He Plays with L.T.D. And his name is Miller. They call him "Onion." He's the one with the bald head. I have been your way many times, with one show or another. I knew that you had heard about my being on dope, and so had the girls, so I didn't want to face you all.

Now, things are different. Now I have everything together. I know that may sound funny, coming from someone in a place like this, but it is true. It took me a long time to grow up, but at last it has happened! For me all those fun and games are over. We are not getting any younger. Why don't you think about you, and the girls coming back down here, and let me take care of you?

So when I get out I am going to give Morristown their first nice club. In fact that is already in progress. It's going to be built from the ground up just the way I want it. I won't lie, and say that I don't have anyone, because I do. She is young, but a very nice and mature young lady. She just came out of school and teaching here in Morristown. She wants to get married when I am out, and I feel that she will make a good wife. **The only thing is I don't love her. I still love you and I always will.**

I saw two of the girls when they were down. One looks just like you! From what I have been told, Raven has grown up to be a very beautiful young lady too. I know she can't think too much of me from all the things she has heard. On top of that, I have never done anything for her. Still you tell her for me that I love her very much, and one day soon I will prove it.

I want you to think about what I'm saying. I know that you can't still feel anything for me, but I feel if I am given the chance then I could make you fall in love with me again. Emily, I am not asking you to make up your mind all at once, and maybe you will just laugh at the whole thing. Anyway, I want you to answer my letter. Just getting a letter from you would be a thrill in itself!!!

P.S. Tell Raven I love her.

P.PS. Please write me back and send me a picture of you and the girls.

Love forever, Larry

Look over bad spelling. You know I never could spell.

Smile

****

And after the first letter, they continued to come—sometimes two per day. Like the first, they all promised love, happiness and a life to share together forever as a family.

At the end of seventh month, Larry joined me in California. At the end of third week, I awoke and became aware that I was in a bed surrounded by rails. I had been in a deep sleep. My eyes focused on a man standing over me, with his arms resting on the rails which surrounded my bed. He held a Bible in his hands. I looked at him for a moment and turned my head away—drifting off again. When I did become aware that I was awake, I discovered a tube ran up my right nostril and down into my throat.

The man with the Bible was gone and now two females stood, one on each side of the rails surrounding the bed I lay in, one leaned down; she called me by my name twice, "Emily Phifer, Emily Phifer." I squeezed my eyes at first closing them again when the light from the room filtered in.

A second passed, I opened my eyes and tried to focus upon the whiteness of the room. One of the females began to tug at the tube with both hands that ran up into my nostril and down into my throat—finally reaching the end, she pulled it out. The other female stood there with a cup and a pitcher of water. "Here, she said. "You need to drink all of it." She pushed an electronic button to raise the head of the bed, handed me the cup filled with water, and watched me drink it in small gulps. She filled it again and kept repeating it until the pitcher which she held was empty. Afterwards, I immediately drifted off to sleep again.

I awoke some hours later, it became apparent that I was in a hospital and something horrible had happened. This time, it was to the sound of Ruth, my oldest sister's voice. She and I reached for each other in desperation for closeness like no other time. My brown eyes melted, and the tears flowed like a waterfall as we held on to each other tightly—the sight and the touch were overwhelming. I had not seen my oldest sister for six years.

For me in a small amount of time and space, as we held on to each other, the events, which led to this moment, began circling through my mind like a fog. I wondered how I, a recent college graduate with a degree in English from the local university, at age thirty-two, a single mother of four teenager children had become such a failure. We did not let go for a long time.

When we did release each other, I was happy and ashamed. I was happy to have my sister with me, to answer a cry for help that until now I did not know I was making; I was ashamed of my failure too—of not dying. I had prepared for a better life. I had prepared mentally to leave this hell. My mind drifted back to the night I took the pills. I was so fatigued from raising children alone, working and going to school. Every single turn was mine. I was fatigued from being separated from *any* relatives; my parents lived three thousand miles away on the East coast. I felt that I had been on automatic pilot my entire life until the first semester of my last year in college when I completed my studies at the university; I was in so much mental pain from years of neglect and abuse—mentally, physically and emotionally from Walter, who my parents married me off to at the tender age of fifteen, someone they nor I did not know at all— we only knew he lived with his parents up the street and up the hill. I was in such despair, I often asked God what had I done; it seemed no one that mattered gave a damn about me. *It was unbearable: poverty, neglect, abuse and isolation from an early age until this moment had created in me a desperate desire I felt to become what I thought my parents were not.* I believed I had succeeded.

Then of all things once I managed to miraculously get Walter, that serious problem that wouldn't go away, off my back and out of my life, negativity came knock, knock, knocking at my door again; this time in the form of Larry, writing promised in his letter he knew he was unable to keep.

For some immature reason, I thought I needed to give Larry a chance because he was Raven's father; I later realized it was too late; he was almost as bad as Walter. He wasn't physically abusive; he was mentally and emotionally abusive. He was still chasing rainbows: spending his gullible unsuspecting parents' hard earned money, talking about going into business and what *we* could do. He had not changed one iota. In his letters everything he said he did—I soon discovered they were still a part of his life. I came to realize he was a pathetic *"leaner."* His intentions were to rely on me and my stability, since I had just completed college with a four year degree and destined for a steady paying job teaching school. Larry was still hooked= *using.* I could not believe that I had fallen for his BS—nonsense, lies and exaggeration once again in my life; I believed his lies at fourteen and now as an adult. Talk about being naïve, I was the queen.

After joining me in the Valley, among some other irresponsible behaviors, finally, one night he literally showed his ass—kicked in the door where we lived and I told him to get out. I was so devastated, isolated, and hurt--that night, I loaded my .38 Smith & Wesson and made several attempts to hold it up to my temple. But I was afraid there would be too much pain. I was unsuccessful. Then there were the pills, which I received from the university doctor—amphetamines, barbiturates and some others--I was having a lot of trouble sleeping—*at night when I finally fell into bed I was even too tired to sleep*. I would lie there thinking about what needed to be done and for whom the next day.

There must have been thirty-five or forty pills. I just wanted to sleep—forever. I didn't want to feel the pain. I swallowed the pills, three, then four at a time, and finally they were all gone. I smiled to think of rest. I laid my head down on a pillow and thought only pleasant thoughts. I remembered drifting off. I remembered thinking that I wouldn't be discovered until it was too late, and that was the way I believed I wanted it. The girls would be at church all day. They were all practically grown and didn't seem to need me anymore. I thought, after all I left my mother's care at age fifteen and tried to raise four children on my own. I just wanted to rest to feel some peace.

And now here I lay. I tried desperately to put the pieces of my life together.

The experiences with Larry and me on the West Coast and all of the events that actually happened…are still somewhat of a blur..! I've tried to recount and tell the story in *Sequel*.

****

Faith Local Mental Health Center
22577 Ridge Street
Mountainview, CA 91356

Telephone 885-2244
Please reply to:
P.O. box 789 Mountainview, CA 91325

Department of Public Social Services
11111 Ban View Blvd.
Mountainview, California 91345
Re: Emily Phifer

Dear Sir:
Emily Phifer was referred to this facility on March 22,
1978 by the Mountainview Memorial Hospital Intensive
Care Unit.   Patient had been admitted to the
Mountainview Memorial Hospital as an attempted
suicide by overdose. Due to the circumstances of her
hospitalization, a psychiatric evaluation was completed
by Dr. Anderson of this facility.

DYNAMIC IMPRESSIONS

Ms. Phifer is experiencing an acute situational
depression. There are several precipitating factor: years
of abuse; isolation, a lack of emotional and financial
support; and the termination of a significant primary
relationship. Apparently these event elicited feeling of
severe depression as evidenced by the seriousness of her
suicide attempt. Her crisis occurred at a particularly
significant time as she recently graduated from college
and thus experienced a change of lifestyle.   The
depression was manifested by self-doubt, isolation and
mild psychomotor retardation.   Though no longer
suicidal, the patient is still in crisis. Ms. Phifer is
otherwise alert, oriented four times, with no evidence of
hallucinations or thought disorder.

RECOMMENDATION

It is recommended that this patient not return to work until she is through her present crisis. Her tolerance for stress is low at the present time. Ms. Phifer has agreed to outpatient therapy to work through her feelings of depression and suicidal ideation. Given her mental and emotional status, this patient should be ready to resume work in three months.

Yours very truly,
Bill McClinton, MSW

Commentary on Emily's Blues by the author

Connie Williams

*W*riting from experience can cause the audience to question motives. And it can be an even more inquisitive matter when the characters are relatives and friends who are still living. They may not perceive events in the same manner as the writer does.

*Y*ou take a risk, but it's a risk with a vision. We take the risk to, hopefully make life better; and therefore, it is a good risk—one taken to improve our country—one taken to open diverse cultural awareness—to share life experiences of social, economical and political histories.

A famous writer once said: write the truth as you know or remember it and let the chips fall where they may.

Retrospectively looking back at my parents' behavior, back then *when I didn't know what I didn't know,* perhaps before age thirty-five, I regarded, in the story, Thomas and Martha's behavior as outrageous, and for a time there was so much shame and disgust directed at them. Most children at a certain age experience something they find disgusting about their parents.

But as we mature and progress pass the frontal lobe development, we experience our own relationships, and view life in a more gregarious cultivation of occurrences; we realize that in most primary relationships, whether it is black, white or other— regardless of the cultural ethnicity (beliefs, norms and practices of a particular group), there will, and there exist discord and many times, it isn't a pretty sight. There is one thing I do know, I cannot blame my parents for all the occurrences that transpired in my life. I choose to give them the benefit of the doubt; consequently, I believe they did the best that they could under the circumstances.

Even in my view of the Phifers in the novel, once I became exposed to their environment, there was a type of relationship disharmony, which extended beyond the boundaries of simple arguments. So I discovered that my parents were not much different when it came to considering the institution of marriage and of "managing their affairs and getting along with one another" twenty-four-seven, theirs was no different than any other marriage that we see from the outside looking in.

In the final analysis, I truly believe longevity certainly has its role—the longer couples remain together, then they are sometimes able to outlive the conflict, unless there is obviously a condition of mental illness. In later years, of course these negative behaviors subsided and were less frequent. I recognized that Thomas and Martha, in the novel and real life, did love each other, raised responsible children—were committed to each other and managed to have a marriage lasting beyond sixty-five years.

*W*riting from experience can also be somewhat difficult—most of us do not take notes as we live our daily lives, so it is necessary to rely on our memory – recollection of time, place and events.   There is a drawback—one can find him or herself caught up in reliving the occurrences and all of the emotions that belong to the experiences.   I had a real arduous and challenging time with present / past tense. It is easy to slip in and out of the present to the past and vice versa, which can cause the work to undergo numerous revisions—this can delay productivity and publication.

*M*ost publishers, it appears, promote high quality—but not everything that is high quality is necessarily the greatest works.   For example, not everything Bach did was wonderful.

*F*unding Muddy Waters' down-home Chicago blues genre unimaginable for the Mississippi Delta artist whose music became unissued for decades. Gordon, Robert and Morgan Nevelle, ***American Masters***, "Muddy Waters: Filmmaker Interview" (1977), but, I believe, with a carefully orchestrated plan, there could have possibly been a greater, perhaps another Muddy Waters.

*T*his story—these experiences had to be told— Emily's story—the situation with teenagers in 1959 and in 2016, in the twenty-first century is real.   In Union

County, the school system where the book was used, teenagers and adults found the story with all of its elements true-to-life, relevant, and it led to important inquiry and discussions that are a part of the universal themes of the human experience.

*W*hen the late Alex Haley, author of ***Roots*** and ***The Autobiography of Malcolm X,*** read ***Emily's Blues,*** he marked a section and called it his favorite because it contained what he considered "good paragraphs." (Part I). He further commented, "You really have a story to tell."

*I*n Part II of Emily's Blues, Emily meets Larry, her first boyfriend, who is responsible for her reluctantly receiving a first kiss at age fourteen. When I taught the tenth grade at Piedmont High School, I remember a student I will call LaSandra, who confessed to me an incident she experienced when a boy at school, whom I will call Marty said to her, "Don't you think it's about time for us to kiss?" These occurrences in Emily's life happened in 1959; it's happening today. It caused Emily to ask: What if I had the wisdom of my parents given to me in their advice. What if I were instructed to say "No!" to both Larry and Walter?

Author's Notes

Allow me to express my sincerest gratitude to Almighty God for his love and protection of my children during this time. For without Him, I have no doubt that we would have fallen along the way. Being close to Him provided the strength to persevere in spite of all the obstacles.

Thanks also to my parents who are no longer with us, who must have done something right, and to the late Mrs. Phifer who, I am sure, had no idea the impression she had made upon me. Thanks to all individuals who believed enough in me to either advise or shelter my children and me. I love you Dawn, and Carrie who are now in Heaven. I am also thankful to the late Johnny, the late Aunt Lynette, Wilma and PC.

ABOUT THE AUTHOR

Connie Williams is a retired Charlotte Mecklenburg Schools high school English teacher. She is a published author of poetry novels and prose. In 1989, she received her Master of Education Degree from the University of North Carolina at Charlotte where she later became a part-time lecturer of English Composition and Rhetoric. In 1996, while a Fellow at Headlands Center for the Arts, in Sausalito, California, she wrote *Emily's Sequel,* part two of *Emily's Blues* (expected publication, 2019*).* It was also at Headlands where she began her second novel *Green,* published in 2015. The Headlands Fellowship was generously funded by the North Carolina Arts Council and the National Endowment for the Arts. In 2016 Williams completed a fourth novel, entitled,   *Jon   and   Lale's Dance,* and currently she has completed an inspirational testimony expected in 2018 and her first children's story. She resides in North Carolina with her husband.